AF365039

H. P. Perlowski

NIGHTMARES UNDER THE MANSION

NIGHTMARES UNDER THE MANSION

Prologue.

He opened his eyes, which radiated scorched pain.
An impenetrable abyss surrounded him. He tried to move his
tense muscles, but they refused to obey. The only movement he
managed to make was twisting his mouth from the effort.
His legs were immobile, with tendons hardening and calves
tensing as if poised to jump. Nothing. Limp in the darkness, he
grunts to force a sound, but the lump in his throat and dry tongue
make it difficult. A faint whine emerges from him. A voice, that
sound of which was so unfamiliar now. He thought about
paralysis, but that wasn't it. "Miners. Maybe I was buried?"
he thought. The turbulent sea of his mind calmed into a peaceful
lake. Despite exerting every ounce of willpower, his body
remained an unyielding prison, with no finger moving to twitch.
He felt drops trickling down his furrowed forehead and other
drops running down his cheeks. There was nothing he could do
to break the helplessness that crushed him. "If only I could know
what happened," he thought. Warmth filled his chest and surged
to his head. He felt the tension in his muscles vanish, replaced by
a delicate tingling that emerged in his back. It spreads over the
rest of the body from the spine, sticking to it like resin.
A gentle calmness settled across his features, softening every line

into a portrait of unwavering serenity. He closed his eyes. The memory of his beloved Natalie filled his mind. The day before yesterday, they made love at her apartment. Then they lay there gazing at each other. Natalie's soft, oval face, with a small nose, full lips, and short blue hair, he loves to mess up. He wished he had her in this place with him. Here. Cold raced through him. Eyelids quivered. He remembered. Mansion. Photos. Natalie. She will look for him. His larynx tensed. He let out a scream that echoed throughout the dark place. It was the last thing he managed to do, then succumbed as soothing warmth and bliss again enveloped him. He drifted to sleep.

Chapter One.

Lamps hung motionless from the ceiling, casting warm lights upon wooden tables and chairs below. The golden glow merged with the mahogany brown of the interior. A blue-haired woman leans at the counter on a high stool. In front of her rests an almost empty bottle of "Shub-Niggurath Dark Dunkel," soft reflections creep across the glass sides. Deep in the room, two men are engaged in discussion, and their gestures throw long shadows on the mahogany wall. Music, conversation sounds, and the clatter of dishes surround the place. The ringing of the telephone jolts the woman out of her daydreaming.

- Hello? - she said.

- Hi Natalie, this is Charlotte Amara - the voice on the other line introduced itself.

Natalie's eyebrows lifted, creating a few small wrinkles on her forehead.

- Oh, hi. How can I help you? - Natalie said.

- I have two things for you. One. Have you received the transfer yet?

- Yes, this morning. Thanks for the rush - She took the bottle to examine how much beer was left.

- Great! Second thing. I mentioned your fantastic paintings to a friend who needs illustrations for his next book.

When we last met, you said you wanted to move away from children's book illustrations - she said.

   - Yes, that's right.

   - Exactly! And his books are socially engaged, intelligent horror novels. His name is Woodrow Camoran. You should hear from him within the next few days.

   - That's great, thank you. I appreciate it - Natalie said.

   - No problem. Once again, many thanks for your beautiful illustrations. Bye.

   - Oh, bye - Natalie said.

Closing her fingers around the bottleneck, she tilts it and drinks the remaining liquid. Natalie's face brightens as the drink's c omplex notes create symphonies on her tongue. Her attention wanders, and eyes glance down to her clothes—a white T-shirt and tight black pants. Dim lighting dances across the fabric, hiding and revealing shadows. Her fingers move to wipe the stains her mind imagines—an unconscious ritual of self-presentation. She grabs the phone again. Quick fingers type a message that will travel through an elusive space. Lines form at the corners of her mouth, a subtle upward curve that hints at shared secrets and anticipation of what will come. When she taps "send," she regrets that a simple text message cannot convey all her feelings. The bartender takes the empty bottle with an almost invisible movement. His face was angular and sharp, with a prominent jawline, cheekbones, and piercing blue eyes.

- You're writing to Daniel - he said.

Natalie's cheeks flushed a soft pink.

- How do you know, Harry?

His eyes gleamed with artfulness and attention.

- You always smile like that when you write to him or talk about him.

She raised her hands in mock surrender, a grin breaking across her face.

- Well, you got me - Natalie said. - Eyes around the head, huh.

Harry leaned against the bar, a smile playing at the corners of his mouth.

- That's part of a bartender's job - he said. - Can I get you anything else? - he said.

Natalie considered for a moment, then nodded.

- I was thinking about a "Yog-Sothoth Oak-aged Vanilla Stout."

- Excellent choice. One "Yog-Sothoth Oak-aged Vanilla Stout" is coming right up.

As the bartender left, Natalie turned her attention to the phone. A subconscious impulse makes her check her messages. The bright screen has nothing to inform her on the subject. The pub filled with background narration disappears as Natalie's thoughts focus on the absent message. The bartender returns with a beer.

- Thanks, Harry - she said.

- If you need anything else, call me - he said, walking away towards the other two customers.

The tar-colored liquid sparkled at her, illuminated by soft overhead lights. In the depths of her eyes, a mixture of sympathy and concern glowed like distant stars, and each hoped for the reaction to decide the future.

- Damn, this "Yog-Sothoth Oak-aged Vanilla Stout" is good - she said. While savoring her beer, she exchanged a few more words with Harry. She drank, said goodbye, and left.

***

She moved with elastic grace, drawing nearer to her apartment, a beloved hermitage in the bustling city. The remaining alcohol wrapped her senses in a subtle bubble, beating with a gentle background noise beneath her skull. It joined her as a well-known song hummed without knowing. Anticipation ran through her veins, a mixture of eagerness and satisfaction. Daniel's presence shone as a beacon for her, guiding her to the right course she craved. The intensity of their feelings stayed strong even though more than two years passed. For her, it grew more and more.

The memory of his touch lingered, a caress beyond the physical. The contours of his arms embraced her in a way she could not describe, and a smile came to her lips. She met Daniel at 35 after surviving several painful relationships, each like a torture chamber. He was more than a man to her. He was a sign of hope after despair. Natalie yawned. "Strange, I felt very bored all of a sudden," she thought.

As she walked down the street, the sunlit glass windows of shops and cafes filled every available space on the ground floor of the buildings, passing by benches and tables along the street.

She walked by the bakery, where the aroma of baked bread wafted through the air. Next to it was a pub with a Polish name, which she visited when Harry had no room left. Daniel had told her once what the name of that place meant. "Something about the mountains?" she wondered. A few minutes later, Natalie saw the familiar, flickering neon sign of "Division Street Booze" casting a dim glow on the sidewalk. The place presented her with choices that were as challenging as they were alluring.

Bottles on the shelves were always welcoming as a group of old friends. The mellow air mingled with the faint scent escaping as someone exited the store. For a moment, the familiar clink of glass bottles and the low hum of a conversation from inside tugged at her, stirring a cocktail of nostalgia and a pinch of regret.

***

She reached N Wood St. From one of the open windows, repeated loud music resembling the work of a jackhammer poured onto the street. She entered her apartment. Three rooms featuring a dedicated painting studio. The walls adorned a timeless coat of white. The living room boasted a sofa, a sleek glass table, and shelves stacked with books. A spacious window ushered in the sun's golden tendrils, crawling through the room just as a curious guest's gaze would wander. Having completed her post-return chores, Natalie sank into the sofa that creaked beneath her. The phone remained blank, devoid of any new message notifications.

Her eyes fixed on the rectangular brightness, lips
curling into a crescent shape. Her fingers glided across the screen,
dialing the desired caller's number. After a few beeps, the artificial
voice suggests recording a message. "Who even bothers with
voicemail anymore?" she thought before sending him another text.
"Hey, honey. Call me :*" Color flushed across her cheeks. Biting
her lip, she stared at the screen when her fingers hovered over the
familiar EMOJI keyboard. Despite her disdain for them, the habit
was hard to break.

From the neighbor's apartment, she heard the opening of
"Denver, the Last Dinosaur." The goofy Denver, zooming on a
skateboard. He could wear sunglasses and ride like a pro but was
still a living fossil.

***

She wakes up, feeling a throbbing pain in her head. "Fuck," she
groaned, dragging herself off the couch. On the table beside her
stands an open bottle of whiskey accompanied by a glass,
inseparable like Scully and Mulder. She glanced at the time and
then at her phone. "New message." Short information quickened
her heartbeat, matching the pain in her head. She checked her text.
"Night RTV promotions, up to 60% off." Natalie deleted it with a
sigh and headed for the shower. Cool water cascaded over her
body. Each stream brought welcome relief, washing away the
numbness that had clung to her like crust.

Chapter Two.

Children's laughter filled the neat, well-furnished room, where
toys lay scattered on the floor. A man sat in a broad armchair
with a child climbing on his back and another on his lap.
He swung a toy above their heads, making them wave their arms
and giggle. He smiled at them, his prominent jawline and slightly
pointed chin giving him a handsome look. The little boy pulled
his ruffled brown hair. "Daddy, daddy, play with us!" they cried.
The laughter and screams of joy faded as a pretty, plump
woman with blond hair curling at her shoulders entered the room.
Her eyes gazed under her bangs at them.

- My larks, give daddy a break - she said.
She walked towards the man and handed him the phone.

- Your sister called.

- Thanks - he takes the phone from her and kisses her on the
cheek. He went to another room and dialed a number.

- Hi Nat, what's up? - he said.

- I can't contact him! We were supposed to meet today. But he
doesn't answer - Natalie said.

- Slow down, sis. Is it about Daniel?

- Two days ago, Daniel went to take photos on the outskirts of
Gary. He should have returned yesterday, and we were supposed

to meet today. I tried to contact him, but he didn't answer. Something could have happened to him!

  - Okay, calm down. Have you tried calling his mother or sister?

  - Yes, Ethan, I tried. Lucy hadn't seen him in a month, and his mother didn't answer the phone.
Can I ask You for something? - Natalie said.

  - Yeah?

  - Will you go with me to his apartment?

  - Now? - Ethan said.

  - Yes. I can't wait any longer! I'm afraid to go there alone in case ... incase something happens to him.

  - Okay, Nat. I'll go with you. Are you at home?

  - Yes - Natalie said.

  - All right. I should be there in about 40 minutes.

  - Thank you, little brother. Thank you. You're the best.

  - Aaaha, see you later - he said and hung up, rubbing his neck.

***

Daylight filled the car's clean cabin, and blurry shapes of other vehicles passed them by. Natalie rolled down the window, unable to bear the smell of the air freshener any longer. A breeze crept over her head, moving her hair. They arrived at the apartment on N Paulina St. They stood in front of the door, Natalie's shaking hands fumbling with her backpack for the keys. A metallic rattle in the hallway confirmed that she had succeeded.

She unlocked the door and let them in.

Natalie turned on the lamps that showed a modern interior with walls hung with various-sized portraits, industrial landscapes, and several photos of her and Daniel. Natalie dashed to the bedroom and from there to the darkroom. She came out after a while, turning her tear-filled eyes to Ethan.

- He's not here - she said. - I'll call him again.
Ethan studied the photos, looking from one to the other.
He lingered on one image, picturing his sister and Daniel in a hug. They smile at the viewer. "He sure knows how to take great photos," Ethan thought. A faint noise caught his attention, and Natalie stood beside him. Her eyes
were wide and watery, bore into Ethan's. He frowned and walked closer to her.

- You want to go to Gary, right? - Ethan said.

- Please, we can get there in an hour by car. With the CTA, it'll take forever! - she said, running fingers through her hair.

- Maybe we'd better call the police?

- No! There's no time for that. Please. If we leave now, you'll be back before supper.

- Nat, I want to help you and am concerned too. But driving aimlessly through Gary won't solve anything. Do you even know what's happening there? - he said.

- We don't have to. I know where he's supposed to be - she said, reaching her phone. The screen bathed her face in white and blue light as she muttered something under her nose while her fingers tapped across the screen. She turned the phone toward him, revealing a black-and white, blurry image of an old mansion.

- Here - she said.

Chapter Three.

A car glides along the highway; an almost empty road stretches before them, and they watch many more cars passing them on the opposite side. Ethan keeps his eyes on the speedometer, which shows 63 miles. Above the road, billowing white clouds darken in the distance, hiding the blue sky. A motorbike rushes by them in the other lane, piercing both ears with its noise. Ethan murmurs a curse. A green square sign on the right side of the road announces Gary.

***

A statue of the city's founder welcomes them, along with the magnificent city hall building. Next to it stands an equally impressive courthouse. Both buildings, built in the neoclassical style, draw attention with their massive, angular shape, many windows, colonnades, and golden domes shining in the sun. They turn onto Washington St. After a few minutes, Ethan's eyes widen at the sight of the building rising behind the ordinary urban structures. The old Neo-Gothic Methodist Church rises above the other buildings, a monument to a bygone era.
Its presence dominates the landscape, a historical giant that does not fit in, as if someone pasted it on.

As they drove closer, they saw how much the church had decayed. The roof, only a shadow of its former self, hangs unsteady. A lonely window holds the remains of the glass panes that fill it, defying the inevitable passage of time. Ivy stretches its tendrils along one of the walls, clinging to the stone.
"Nature is taking over what was once created by human hands, Natalie thought." The graffiti stretches on the walls, clashing with the sacred character of this place. The fence, damaged in many places, fails to stop intruders from entering, and portals that the faithful once crossed, now crumbled and cracked, look like gates to the depths of oblivion.

- How the hell did this happen? - Ethan said. Natalie looked at him in surprise, as if she hadn't heard the question.

- I don't remember exactly, but after 197-something, the number of churchgoers diminished, and they lost interest in the holy place - she paused for a while. - Three weeks ago, Daniel and I went inside. It was even worse there. After that, he had the idea to make a photo report about 'dying buildings,' as he called it."

- That sounds like a good idea.

- Yeah. He was very excited about it - a flicker of a smile crossed her lips but disappeared fast.
She watched the church shrink in her eyes as they drove away.

***

Ethan switched on the radio, glancing at his sister. He sighed. Anchorman began talking about criminal activity, so he changed to the music station, and a soft melody filled the car.
Natalie turned to him.

- Did Mary mind that I suddenly dragged you out of the house? - she said.

- I told her it was a family matter. She understood. But the kids miss you. They want to see their 'paint aunt' again.

- That's nice - she pulled a hip flask from her backpack and drank. Warmth flowed through her chest, soothing her chaotic thoughts.

***

They left Gary's main streets behind and drove through the narrow roads of the city's outskirts. At one point, they saw a smooth gray wall rising from the road to the sky, mixed with dark blue clouds. A matte barrier obscured everything they could see. Natalie felt a chill run down her spine as they approached the fog. They drove closer until the wall of fog consumed them. The road disappeared in a veil of fog. Sunlight struggled to break through the thicket that had fallen on them, turning the world into a gray void. A blur of faded asphalt, swallowed by a hungry embrace, while the headlights battled, cutting faint arcs in the emptiness. Their efforts had little effect beyond the hood of the car.
The fog brought a silence that muffled the driving sounds, and the trees seemed like phantoms appearing only to disappear behind them.

Water vapor clung to the glass, reducing visibility, and the wipers moved back and forth, painting abstract streaks that obscured any trace of the real landscape. Firms, Ethan's hands held the steering wheel. The cocoon of gray around them made the world seem not to exist beyond unpenetrable fog. Minutes and seconds blended into an unimaginable continuum that prevented them from measuring the space traveled. Speed lost meaning as if forward motion had no effect in this suspended reality. Every action demanded increased concentration in this world of fuzzy features and muted shapes. The fear of hidden dangers lurking just beyond the limited field of vision heightened the senses, turning driving into a delicate dance of caution and determination. As they drove through the fog, forgotten houses appeared on both sides.

The entrances without doors led to dark and silent interiors. They haunted Natalie with their empty windows, watching her like eye sockets. She saw the decay of roofs, facades, and walls and felt like an intruder in this necropolis.

They passed by one of the abandoned houses. Tattered curtains swayed in the windows, a false sign of life. Time had destroyed the house's distinctiveness, softening its edges and corners—the picture of misery bound by a common fate of abandonment. Wild vegetation was growing rampantly. Untrimmed grass, bushes, branches, and vines covered the place. A bicycle lay crumpled on the porch, mud and rust covering its frame. The swings in a forgotten playground move like someone is still using them.

Natalie hears their creaking in her mind. Houses once filled
with life exude quiet resignation as if accepting their fate.
The mist clings to them, protecting the secrets they hold.

   - We're almost there - she said.

***

Ethan exhaled, pressing his head into the headrest. With its
female voice, the GPS delivered the news: they had reached their
destination. Driving through the dense fog, even during daylight,
sapped his energy and added stress. Not being familiar with the
area compounded his unease. He felt Natalie's hand on his
shoulder as he rubbed his hands, trying to get rid of the numbness
in his fingers. He looked up at her face, full of concern.

   - Hey, are you okay? - she said.

   - Yeah, just give me a minute, and I'll be ready - he said.
The asphalt road ended and was replaced by tall grass of vast
fields bathed in the everpresent fog. Natalie didn't like leaving the
car and continuing on foot, but it was the only way to reach the
mansion. Goosebumps covered her hands as she exited the vehicle.
She grabbed the khaki field jacket from the back seat and put it on.
The rough material slid over her skin, falling on her shoulders.
She rolled the sleeves above the wrists and turned up the collar,
cutting off the air around her neck. She touched the collar and
inhaled the scent of the owner. "As soon as I find you, I'll finally
return it to You," she thought. Ethan slammed the car door and
stared from behind it.

- I need to stretch my legs - he said.

She nodded. He walked away, his footsteps rustling in the grass. She grabbed her backpack and checked the phone. One bar range. No WI-FI nearby. The screen showed a 19% battery charge. She grimaced, cursing herself for not charging it before leaving.

- Natalie! Here! - Ethan said. She turned her head. He was a dark shape in the distance. She felt a heaviness in her stomach and a coldness on her forehead. Her legs refused to move, her knees knocking together.

- It's a car! I think it's Daniel's! - he said.

Tears streamed down her cheeks, pale as the fog around them. She walked towards the car, feeling stones under her feet. Ethan was next to it, staring. The silver of the vehicle was unmistakable.

- It's Daniel's car - Natalie said.

She ran to the driver's door, but the car was empty. Locked doors stay unmoved by her efforts to open them. She looked at the glass, the hood, the paint, searching for any sign of an assault or accident. There was none. "He saw the end of the road and continued on foot," she thought. She dialed his number, but it went to voicemail.

Natalie leaned against the car's hood with her hand on her chest. Ethan came out of the fog from where his car was. She noticed large black cylinders of flashlights in his hands.

- Here, take it - he said.

- Thanks. That will be useful - she said and flipped the switch, and the object shot out a light beam.

- We should get going.
Ethan nodded, and they set off. Wild grass touched the knees, and from time to time, they stopped to look at their feet. The crunch of stones and cracking sticks announce their every step.
Natalie stops. The glow of the phone illuminated her face. She raises her eyebrows, eyes following something on the screen.
- We're close - she raised her hand, pointing ahead. - We have to move in this direction - she said.
- Okay - he said, rubbing his knee.
Even though it didn't seem possible, the fog thickened, becoming a milky suspension, overwhelming their bodies and thoughts. Somewhere in the distance, she heard a dog barking, the first sound that was anything other than crunching beneath their feet. As they went deeper, the crunching sounds accompanying their steps began to turn into mud splatters. On their way, they encountered a tree with leafless branches twisting in different directions.
- There's a lake nearby. That's why the fog is so damn heavy here - Natalie said.
She tried to sound casual like it was an ordinary hike.
But she couldn't stop thinking about Daniel.
She imagined him waiting for her, holding her hand, kissing. She reassured herself that nothing terrible had happened and his absence would be a misunderstanding they would laugh about later at Harry's counter. She chattered her teeth as she switched the flashlight to her other hand and tucked her free hand into the pocket.

The splash of leaves mixed with mud squelched in rhythm around them. The teeth chattered again. Maybe it was the fog or cold that penetrated her body from all sides, but Natalie's mind was attacked by thoughts that she kept pushing away. As if they had found a hidden way and were beginning to spread, poisoning not only the mind but also the soul.

"Maybe he wasn't here at all. Maybe he ran away with another? With that redhead Lucy, for example," she thought. Her breathing didn't quicken. Blood didn't boil in her veins. It had no physical effect on her. She didn't believe these thoughts but couldn't get rid of them anymore. "Where's the damn house?" - she thought.
The grass brushed against her legs, leaving wet marks on her pants. A guide through the fog and, at the same time, a reminder of the unpredictability of the nature they walk on. Ethan stopped a few steps ahead of her, peering into the fog as if he expected to see someone in it. Ethan raises his hand to stop her.

- Listen - he said.
Natalie lowered her head, closed her eyes, and felt a twitch in her spine. The contents of the backpack became heavier.
She listened to the emptiness surrounding them, but nothing but the rustle of the grass reached her ears. She spread her arms, looking at him and opening her mouth to let out a whine when she heard it. Discussion.

Somewhere nearby, human voices break through the fog. They exchanged glances, and Ethan shook his head. Natalie held her breath as she heard the voices getting louder and their owners getting closer.

- I'm sure we're dealing with another cryptid specimen now.
It can't be the same one as in 1887 - man said.
 - Yes, but are we dealing with a pup, or was it always a tribal
system? Behaviors known from some encounters indicate a tribal
structure - a woman said.
The man's voice held a note of caution.
 - Be careful, my dear. You realize it's not that simple - man said.
Figures emerge from the fog and stand before Natalie and Ethan.
Natalie moved back, creating some distance. The woman in front
of them gasped, covering her mouth. Natalie studied the woman's
oval face, smooth brown skin, petite nose, and almond eyes. Her
black hair was pulled back in a tight bun. She glanced at the man
next to her, who smiled at them. He had a square face and hazel
eyes that intrigued her. His dark blond hair was combed and
sprinkled with gray at the temples.
 They were both dressed in overalls with a camouflage pattern,
stuffed backpacks hanging from behind their shoulders.
Bulging pockets, black straps with bags, and camera cases hanging
rom the ends. The woman also carried a tripod over her shoulder.
They remind Natalie of hardcore
preppers prepared for the end of the world. The man raised his
hand in greeting, and a pair of binoculars swung from his neck.
 - Hello, forgive our surprise, but we didn't expect to meet
anyone here. Especially in this weather - man said.
 - Are You lost? - woman said, approaching them.
 - Yes! Are you from here? Do you know the area? - Natalie said.
She was blushing when she heard her trembling voice.

- Oh! Then we'll be happy to help - woman said and turned to the man.

- Right, Fin?

- Of course. This is my wife, Maya, and my name is Fintifluch, but you can call me Fin. We are cryptozoologists.

- Cryptozoologists? Do you study dead animals? - Ethan said, frowning. Fin chuckled and shook his head.

- No, no, it's something completely different. Let me explain - then Maya smiled and tapped her husband on the shoulder.

- Sorry, he's a real aficionado. Are you looking for Kassogtha's mansion?

- We're looking for an old mansion, but I don't know its name - Natalie said. - We're looking for my fiancé. He went there to take photos.

The phone flashed, and Daniel's face appeared on the screen. The cryptozoologists stared at the screen, Fintifluch's eyes wandering over the image.

- No, sorry - Maya said.

- But we can help you with the Kassogtha's mansion - Fintifluch said.

Breaking branches and the clatter of stones accompanied their steps again. They felt the hard ground under their boots.

- We're going there later too. To the mansion. But first, we want to check some mysterious holes in the ground that we spotted from the drone - Fintifluch said.

- You have a drone? Cool - Ethan said. His face shines.

- Yes. Despite the fog, Dantès is still quite helpful - Fintifluch said.

- Dantès?

- Oh, sorry. We called our drone Dantès - he said.

- Yes, and that was my idea - Maya said. She grinned at Ethan.

***

Natalie looked at the others' backs. The backpack seemed to be dragging her down. She ran her tongue across the dry palate, the friction sending shivers down her spine. Cold sweat comes on her fingers. She reached under her jacket and pulled out a hip flask. She tilted her head back and sipped the liquid. She sighed and licked her lips. "Much better," she thought and tucked the hip flask back under her jacket with a clink. Then she joined the others, walking next to Maya.

- What did you say is the name of this mansion? - Natalie said.

- It's not so much the name of the mansion itself but of the family that lived in it - Maya said. - Kassogtha. Gerald Kassogtha commissioned its construction in 1908. He worked for the local steelworks, dealing with what today we would call human resource management. The job required his constant presence, so the property was soon built, and he later brought his family here. And now an interesting fact - Maya raised her finger.

- The last members of the Kassogtha family lived there until 1985 - she said, adjusting one of the bags.

- Few people remember them today, so when someone mentions this place, colorful terms such as "an estate in the fog" or "abandoned residence" are used.

She looked at Natalie, smiling at her.

- Sorry about this info dump - She said.

Fintifluch waved his arms as he rattled about what brought them here. Ethan listened with his mouth ajar and his eyebrows knitted together.

- Michigan...what? - he said. As if not hearing him, Fintifluch continued.

- I know, I know. After so many years of searching, I also began to think that it was just a legend.

- Sorry, but I don't know what it is - Ethan said.

- What! Really? - he said and turned into Maya. - Honey, our friend here doesn't know what Michigan Dogman is.

- Tell him, Fin - she said.

Wet grass crunched beneath their boots with every step.

- In short, it is an amazing creature with a dog's head and a humanlike body. Moves both upright and quadrupedal. It was first sighted in 1887, and there have been numerous encounters with this creature over the years - he said, waving his hands and making circles, punctuating each word.

- 1950, 1976, and beyond, more and more people admit to seeing it. He even attacked some! That's why it can't be one specimen. Too many reports and too many different places. We have been researching this for a long time, and I can tell you with certainty that...

- Sorry, Fin, but I have to interrupt you - Maya said, nodding.

- We're almost there.

A dark shape loomed in the fog, and Natalie stopped.
The throbbing pain in her legs faded into the background as her
heart seemed to expand, and her stomach felt like shrinking.
Numb hands hung along the body, and the cold inside her chewed
through her cheeks as if it wanted to get free.
They approached the nightmare and saw its full horror.

A three-story horizontal block topped with a pointed roof with
more holes than tiles. Chimney remnants now looked more like a
stump sticking out of the corpse. Glassless windows, graffiti,
boards, and garbage piled up beneath the cracked walls.
The contours were rounded and oval, making the building look
like it was melting. A wounded, crawling creature that chose this
ground as its final resting place. Natalie reached for her phone.
"Even if he doesn't answer, maybe we'll at least hear his ringtone,"
she thought.
  - I'm calling - she said, more to herself than to the others.
Voicemail. She moved the phone away from her head, but no
other sound crept in above the rustle of the wind and the tapping
of loose boards. She hung up. Her head rumbled like a drum, her
heart racing. Panting, she turned her gaze toward the
cryptozoologists.
  - Thank You for helping us - she said.
  - You're welcome - Fintifluch said. - Maybe we'll meet again.
But now we need to check these mysterious holes. They look very
promising.
Maya poked him.

- Oh, sorry. Good luck - he said and gave her a smile that showed all his teeth. Then walked away, adjusting one of the clasps. Maya hands fell on Natalie's shoulders, locking eyes with her.

- I hope you find him - she said.

Ethan stood next to Fintifluch.

- Tell me honestly. Have you ever seen any strange creatures like this Michigan Dogman? - he said.

- Yes, we saw. We saw indeed - said Fintifluch.

Chapter Four.

They slipped in through the rear, guided by the remnants of a doorframe. Natalie's whole body quivered, and the knot in her stomach threatened to unleash nausea. Pinpricks of light moved across the walls, unveiling the eerie new world they ventured into. Ethan's flashlights exposed naked brick walls and cracked floors strewn with debris, rot, and grime. A noxious odor, a blend of fruit gone bad and sulfur, permeated the space.

This was their welcoming committee. Tears rose in Natalie's eyes, and a cry echoed throughout the room.

-Daniel! Daniel! - she screamed until she could only whimper. The saliva thickened like glue, and she felt like shellless snails were pushing down her throat. Ethan touched her shoulder.

- Come on, let's check the stairs - he said.
They started walking up the stairs, which creaked, revealing their presence. Ethan frowned, shaking the railing. A shower of dust and rust flakes flew down.

Holes in the walls and the shapes that were once windows allowed the wind to blow through three rooms and the corridor.

- Let's save the battery. It's quite light out here - Ethan said.
The creaking of the floor made Natalie afraid to take another step.

Ethan entered one of the rooms, and Natalie followed him.
Pale daylight poured in through the holes, allowing to see details.
On one of the surviving walls, hanging the rotten wallpaper, the
flowery pattern now resembled the deformed faces of drowned
people. The patch of wallpaper closest to the window twitched
like a broken bird's wing. They did not enter the next room.
They saw its interior through the ribs of vertical and horizontal
wooden beams. The only remaining door on this floor creaked
as Ethan went to the last room.

- Oh fuck - he said. The wooden cradle moved rhythmically,
rocked by the wind in the middle of the room, the blackened
remnants of paint giving the impression of dried blood.
They couldn't tell whether the creaking echoed in their brains
was from the floor or the cradle.

- I bet someone left this here on purpose to scare the shit out of
anyone who walks in here - he said.

They returned to the corridor, and Natalie headed to the next
stairs. Ethan touched her hand.

- Nat, can You wait here? I'll check the next floor - he said.

- What? No! We go together - she said.

- Please, Nat. If it is okay, I call You. Her eyes widened, and she
nodded. The creaking faded away as Ethan disappeared up the
stairs.

The cold of the flask stung her fingers, but the contents warmed her body and numbed her mind. "What if he drove here to meet with someone? And now he's fucking some bitch who doesn't even know who Gauguin was," she thought. "What if Ethan finds him up there, dead?"

She shook her head and took another sip. The boards creaked as she crouched down, hugging her knees, the tremble spreading through her hands. The vision of Daniel cheating on her overshadowed thoughts of his death. It settled in her head and sucked in all the other possibilities. Her eyes burned and pinched her like two stones pressed into her skull. Her lips quivered, and she heard her own voice.

- Please come back. Come back to me. You said you would never leave me, but you did.

Her knees crack as she stands up, looking at the ceiling and dust falling from it. Hushed men's voices broke through from above. She headed for the stairs.

Legs carried her through the ruin that Kassogtha's family mansion had become. She felt as if she were levitating above the stairs, no longer hearing the complaints of the bending wood. She ran into the corridor. Air rushed on her face. The voices stopped as she ran into one of the rooms. Ethan and some man stood in a room full of garbage and caked with filth. His ragged gray beard fell over his chest, and his clothes were as tattered as the building. "Santa Claus in disguise," Natalie thought. Ethan turned around, looking into her eyes and nodding towards the stairs. As they were coming down, Natalie asked about the stranger.

- Homeless. I'll tell you in a moment, just let's go down to the ground floor. Flashlights again accompanied them as Ethan touched her shoulder.

- Daniel was here. He gave that guy two dollars in exchange for telling him about the building - he said.

- And?! Natalie's eyes sparkled in the artificial light.

- He also told him about the basement.

Ethan's fingers rested on the rusty doorknob. Natalie nodded. Gritting his teeth, he opened the door that was scratching against the floor. Thick and suffocating air filled their nostrils, carrying the acrid stench of mold and rot. Two shafts of light wandered around the room. Filth and junk like a broken sofa, a cracked mirror, a torn curtain, and other discarded items were resting in the dark. The shadows gave way to a scene of decay and ruin, revealing it inches by inches. Old and discarded objects lingered there, like they were in purgatory, waiting for someone to show them the next direction of their journey. The clink of the bottle resounded with the force of an explosion in the darkness.

- Sorry, I didn't see that - Ethan said.

Natalie stepped over the obstacles and walked to the wooden desk covered with dust and cobwebs. Underneath, she found a photograph with curled edges that looked like they might break off with a single touch. The sepia tones showed a man, a woman, and three children, with the mansion stretching out behind them.

Blurry faces looked at her with dark spots where their eyes should be. Apart from a few clothing details, the rest blended together.

- Ethan! Look at this! - she said.

A few dings and pops announced his arrival. She pointed with the light at the photo as he stood beside her.

- Kassogth's family, I guess - she said.

- They don't look happy.

Among the lifeless chaos, they sometimes found paths, remnants of someone's attempts to navigate this maze. Natalie's leg hit something. For a second, she didn't feel the floor. Her arms shot through the air. The free hand touched some surface and clamped down. A screeching erupted. Natalie stopped. "Shit, almost," she thought. The light went in search of the culprit.
Just behind her, like a sleeping anaconda, lay a rolled-up carpet.

The air seemed to thicken, pressing down on her and filling her lungs with staleness and dust. Natalie's body trembled.
Her stomach throbbed and growled. She took another step, but an emptiness opened beneath her. The light swirled.
The sensation of the cold nothingness rushed against her.
Her arm brushed against a rough surface. She grabbed it.
A tug on her arm sent pain filling all her nerves. She heard the crack of wood, and the inertia of falling wrapped her again. Ethan headed towards the noise that filled this land of dust and oblivion.

- Natalie!

Scattering bottles, boxes, and other junk, he ran to where she had disappeared. Hitting the floor with his knee, he knelt at the trapdoor, feeling a wooden flap under his hand. Below, a spot of light showed Natalie. Pieces of wood from the broken ladder covered her legs. A green fluff of moss surrounded her on the ground. Ethan extends his hand, lighting the space as best he can. He opened his eyes wider as if that would dispel the darkness filling the corners. Natalie let out a soft grunt, her chest rising with a steady rhythm.

Ethan pulled a plastic bottle from the backpack next to the trapdoor. He poured out water, aiming at her head. The liquid spilled onto the moss, vanishing into the green depths.

- Damn it - he said.

His eyes focused on the target, and the shaking of his hand swirled the bottle's contents. The water splashed onto Natalie's face. A flash of light greeted her open eyes. The back and elbow of her left arm radiated heat, the vibrations of pain stinging like thousands of teeth biting her flesh. She tried to move her bruised arm. She felt a phantom grasp, and then the pain pulsated like a neutron star. She raised her other hand, wiggling her fingers. She bent her elbow, preparing for another pain attack, but it didn't come. A familiar voice cut through the ringing in her ears.

It became clearer each moment until her mind sent her the right signal.

- Ethan? - she said, feeling her teeth vibrate.

She could see a silhouette through the light as if looking at a detuned portable TV screen.

- I'm here! Don't move! - he said.
The sticky goo in her mouth squirted down her throat.
She coughed, and something yankled in her neck. A hot sensation filled her sinuses like wool. Natalie tilted her head, and liver-colored liquid gushed out of her nose. Coldness filled her nostrils. She felt like she had taken the first breath in her life.
"Fuck" her brother's voice rang out in the distance.
- Nat! Look at me!
Ethan's outline came into her field of vision again.
- All right. Listen! Try not to move - he said. - Nat, do you understand?
- Yes.
- All right. Can you tell me where you feel the most pain?
-Fucking everywhere - she said.
A cascade of coughs echoed into the darkness.
- Nat, please listen to me carefully now. All right?
- Yes - Natalie said, feeling saliva thicken again.
- I have to call an ambulance. There's no reception here. I have to go outside. You'll be alone for a moment. All right?
- Yes.
- I'll be back in a moment - he said.
He stood up. A jumping streak of light marked his route.
Sweat beaded the surface of the phone in his hand. Objects and surroundings merged into one. Shapes and details lost their meaning. He smashed everything unlucky enough to get in his way, filling the basement with destruction.
His heart was beating out of his chest in time with his footsteps.

The legs became battering rams, absorbing blows from shelves, chairs, or boxes. Thoughts flooded through his head, as invasive as telesales men. "Goddamn ruin," he kept repeating like a jammed record. His fingers continued to wrap around the phone, transferring heat to it. Everything before his eyes became an abomination of chaos, jerking and swirling. He picked out one point that attracted his frantic gaze. Door.

He climbed stairs that seemed endless. Ethan's foot hit the step, and the wood wailed under the weight of his knees. He stifled a groan as he pushed up to continue climbing. A cool breeze greeted him as he left the basement depths behind him. Panting, he sat on the dirty floor, creaking in protest. He put the flashlight down, his face illuminated by the phone. Fingers moved across the surface. There were a few creaks from behind him. He turned around. A man stood in the back, and Ethan recognized the homeless man through the cover of shadows. Shuffling over the cracked wood, he moved forward. His stiff legs carried him like an animated mannequin. The light creeping in through the holes fell on the man's face. Ethan jumped to his feet and, without turning his head, took a few steps back. Gray fluff covered the man's skin, glistening in the daylight and seeping through holes and gaps. The eyes, whose eyelids were almost invisible, were all white, contrasting with a weathered complexion.
The rugged conjunctivas were like the impastos in Post-Impressionist paintings. Coffee-colored liquid oozed from the parted mouth. The homeless man took a step forward.

A tingling sensation filled Ethan's body, his temples throbbing like a speeding train. Mary and the kids flashed through his mind. He looked around. A shovel covered with a dust sheet lying against the wall. Ethan lifted it and pointed it in front like an ancient weapon from Greek mythology.

- I don't know what's wrong with you, but don't even try to come here!

The homeless man took another step.

- I'm warning you!

Muscles tensed as Ethan raises the shovel, ready to strike. His fingers turned white on the shaft. Zigzags of veins seemed to pulsate in his red face. "Natalie is lying there in some rotten hole. Instead of calling for an ambulance and waiting by her side, I stuck with this weird guy," he thought. "Fucking enough."

- Go back upstairs to your business!

The homeless man took another step.

- Fuck! Turn back, or I will destroy you like Godzilla is destroying Japan!

The homeless man took another step. Stopped. Spasms spread throughout his body, and he fell like a cutdown tree. The scream of cracking wood filled the entire ground floor. A pungent cloud of dust rose into the air. The floor creaked beneath the man's motionless body.

Ethan didn't move. His fingers no longer felt the shovel. Dots of sweat flowed all over his body, not soothing the heat that filled him. Ethan's legs trembled with each step he took toward the man.

- Hey! Can you hear me? Are you dead, or do you want to jump scare me?

The noise in his head drowned everything else. The smell of unwashed flesh, urine, and something his brain couldn't identify reached him. Ethan held his breath as the metal end of the shovel stabbed the fallen man's foot. Nothing. He blew out a breath and stabbed again. Nothing.

The homeless man lay with his arms spread out like for a hug, his head swallowed by the hole made by the fall. The shovel clanged as it hit the floor. He moved away from the body and pulled out his phone. The stillwhitened fingers flexed as if they belonged to someone else. He tapped the same place several times, but the screen did not respond. "Damn touchscreens," he thought.

The homeless man's body twitched. A gurgle filled its insides, and it twitched again. Twisting bulges moved under the dirty T-shirt. A biological danse macabre caught Ethan's eye.
The T-shirt stretched and ripped, revealing a gray-purple stomach. The skin began to pull as tight as the fabric. Ethan felt breakfast rising to his throat. The homeless man's stomach turned into bloody shreds, patches of skin falling in all directions.

Like a volcano, it threw out a gold and red particle cloud. They twinkled in the little light, then swirled and fell, covering everything like ash. Ethan bent over from the grip that seized his insides. His throat vibrated with the cough that tore his lungs. The occiput and sinuses were throbbing. The skin all over his body stung. He hit the boards that blocked the window next to him with a thud. The room blurred as heat filled his eyes. Trembling from coughing fits, he stretched his arms out before him. The opening through which they had entered was now a bright blur. The stair railing creaked as he bumped into it. The inner grip made each breath feel like a hit of a fiery fist.

His legs curled under him, and blood filled his mouth as Ethan's jaw made contact with the floor. He resembled a deep-sea creature washed ashore. His limbs, once so agile and helpful, now betrayed him. He was coughing, spraying red drops. Spheres of his eyes now looked like brush strokes on a canvas. Every part of his body was crying out for a moment of rest. Heaviness expanded as if everything inside him wanted to collapse.

And then, warmth radiated from within his chest, spreading to his limbs. It broke the invisible chains that bound him and melted the weight that had taken over his muscles. Warmth cocooned Ethan's mind like resin. His bloody mouth twisted into a smile, welcoming the unfamiliar feeling. The floor seemed to be molding foam tailored to his shape. The tentacles of dreams wrapped around him and dragged him into the depths of slumber.

Chapter Five.

A click escaped Natalie's jaw as she opened her mouth.

- Ethan!

Her eyes were focused on the outline of a trapdoor. An awful taste filled her mouth, and she leaned her head and spat out red saliva.

- Ethan! - she tried again. Echo was her only companion in this void she found herself in. "He must still be outside," she thought. Time ceased to exist for her as she lay here as if thrown beyond the frames of existence. "It's hard to get here. He has to explain to them," she thought. The building they passed on their way here appeared in her mind—a red-brown behemoth with a glass front and endless rows of windows.

"What was the name of this hospital?" she thought, pushing away another faint. A groan escaped her lips as the pain in her elbow struck again. Lying there, the rest of her body felt numb, almost as if the pain had decided to concentrate on her elbow.

"Daniel is still out there. I must find him", she thought. Flexing her legs, Natalie drew her knees toward her chest. The ladder fragments shifted beneath her without a twinge.

However, when she tried to get up, her back made a grinding sound and several clicks accompanied by the vertebrae skipping.

With a contorted face, she fell onto the moss, which received her like the father of the prodigal son. She lay forlorn, pressing lips together.

A soft splash in the distance reverberated to her consciousness. She listens to this sound, the regularity that fills her with ease. In the apartment, such sounds always felt like someone drilled through her head, and each drop was a thunderclap. Here, it was different. Natalie's thoughts merged with the rhythm of the drop. The alien place vanished. "There is no place like home".
She squeezed her eyes shut, conjuring the image of her bathroom. Blue tiles covered the walls, a cotton rug on the floor, and a silver chrome faucet from which drops fall. One after another.
The smell of a towel, a green hair dryer, and a steamy mirror.
The neighbors' voices through the ventilation square.

Tears came out from under her eyelids when she thought about Daniel again. "Is he also lying there somewhere? Or is he even worse?" "Ethan still didn't come back. Maybe something happened to him too?" she thought, leaning on her good hand. "I'm alone here now, in this dreadful place. I can't wait for him." Her heart began to gallop again.
A metallic grinding drowned out her thoughts. Resonating far above, it reached her with a vibrating echo, disappearing after a second. "Ethan," she thought. Her heart was pounding, but its rhythm had changed, filling her with inner warmth with each beat.
- E t h a n !

The dripping from the distance was pouring into her mind again. Plop. Plop. Plop. Vibrating breath. Heart-rhythm.
She strained her eyes until the trapdoor above her began to sway and shift. The illusion grew, but her eyes remained fixed on that one point, watching for the slightest movement. Plop. Plop. Plop.
Above her, everything returned to its usual dead stillness. Ethan's footsteps didn't fill the basement with a cascade of thuds and cracks. She waited while the water dripped.

Plop. Plop. The whisper of water pulled her from sleep, and the afterimages of her dreams faded, returning to where they came from. Natalie rubbed her eyes, feeling a sticky crust around her elbow. She moved her arm a few times, staring at it as if it had just grown. Natalie's hand cut through the air, painting on a non-existent canvas. Her hands sunk into the moss, her vertebrae popping as she sat down. Her legs went beyond the pool of light, and she groaned, gritting her teeth. "I did it," she thought, rubbing her knees. Another vertebra grated somewhere in her back as she raised the flashlight.
The humid walls gleamed in the light, revealing the meanders of plant forms attached to them. Natalie focused the light on the nearest fragment. The swollen, convex growths cast shadows that magnified their depth. She moved away from what had settled on the walls of this place, but her eyes still wandered around the tangled, fractal shapes—interspersed with orange-brown baggy tubers with lumps of various sizes sticking out of them.

From between, as if crawling, white fleshcolored threads were emerging in different directions. Thick and thin, they disappeared under the tangle of other growths, only to appear above them in another place after a while. Natalie's brain brought up a memory of pale yellow roundworms behind the glass of the display case she had observed during biology classes.

- Ascaris lumbrico... something - she said.
The growths were covered in many places with semi-transparent fluff, shimmering with gold.

It all appeared to Natalie as living, crawling things.
Slimy, pulsating creatures that bite wounds in stone and roam with a purpose known only to them. They started their journey from the floor, moving further and growing in the middle of the wall to disappear into the abyss of the ceiling.
She looked towards the trapdoor.

-Ethan! Ethan!

The weight settled in her chest again, squeezing her lungs. "Something must have happened," she thought. Her shoe hit the remnant of the ladder, which rolled across the soft ground. Her cheeks became wet. Her legs trembled like they were going to fall apart. Darkness clouded her thoughts, bringing to mind the worst images. She tightened her fingers on the flashlight handle and raised her hand like throwing a grenade. Her breathing was as quick as a machine gun as she aimed at the wall covered in biological abominations. She froze in this position.
Plop. Plop. Plop.

The flashlight fell to the floor with Natalie next to it. She was on her knees, shaken by spasms of vomit.

"If something happened to Ethan, I won't help him if I stay here. And what if I find Daniel? Will I be able to help him?" she thought. The decision lit up like a green light, allowing her to cross to the other side. She looked above her, and then she saw it. She stood on her tiptoes, holding out her hand with a flashlight. The strap of the backpack was hanging at the trapdoor. The beam of light flew up and down several times. "It's not that high, but there's no way I can reach it," she thought.

She lighted the floor. A ladder stringer lay among the scattered rungs. Topped with two rungs, it resembled an extended letter "F." She pressed the flashlight into the moss. The wrenched stain of light swept across the trapdoor. The big "F" crackled in her hands, and Natalie stifled a moan as she felt the sting in her fingers. She staggered as the big "F" moved upwards. Her legs pressed into the moss, crushing it into a pulp. She flexed the muscles. The bones clicked, and the wood cracked. A dull thud announced the ex-ladder's contact with the trapdoor. Scraping echoed upwards as she moved the "F" towards her backpack.

Natalie pulled. A crash came to her from above, sending a small cloud down. Hundreds of pricks spread across her face, forcing her to close her eyes.

- Fuck! - she said, wiping her face on her sleeve.

She felt the stiff tendons and vibrating muscles. She pulled again. A few pops at the top.

The big "F" jumped back and hit the with a clunk. She let
go. The ladder stringer remained up, creaking. Her fingers dipped
into the moss, absorbing the coolness of the moisture.
Natalie tried to move them, but they felt like they were carved
from stone. Her hands touched, and the skin friction sent shivers
down the body.
   A bang above her head.
"It's crumpling," she thought and rolled into a corner. With a crash
and an echo-multiplied smash, a piece of the ceiling and the
trapdoor frame collapsed where she had just been crouching.
Curled in a fetal position, she felt dirt in her hair and pieces of
stone on her clothes. A line of ringing formed beneath her skull.
Dust from the dilapidation covered her like a blanket, sending her
into nothingness.

   Natalie wiped the steamy surface, revealing another Natalie
looking at her from inside the circular plastic frame. She wrapped
herself in a terry cloth towel that stuck to her body like a bandage.
The cotton rectangle caressed her feet, absorbing the water
dripping from her hair. She looked for a hair dryer and noticed
the green handle sticking out from the polyester case. Plop. Plop.
She stroked the handle, which gleamed in the halogen light.
Her fingers swelled, and the torn skin revealed flesh and bones
that exploded, splattering across the blue tiles and piercing shot
through her feet. She looked down at the squirmed, nematode-like
mass that covered her legs. They were everywhere, spread over
the walls and the shower cabin.

With each passing second, they consumed her more and more, bringing her closer to the twisted, creeping creatures. Her mouth grimaced with a scream as she disappeared into the depths of the repulsive life. Plop. Plop. Plop.

Plop. Plop. The overwhelming blackness did not dissipate as Natalie opened her eyes, trying to see through the curtain of darkness. Rubble dug into her hands and knees as she climbed an unseen pile. Boards, fragments of bricks, and shards of something metal bit with every movement.

She heard their clatter as they rolled beneath her. One of the angular obstacles caught her pant leg, and she heard ripped cloth. She jerked her foot, and something slid beneath her, taking Natalie too. She rolled down from a pile that cut her arms and back. The spinning motion stopped. Her groan cut through the air, echoing off the jagged surfaces she'd been crawling on. She lay there, sucking in the dust swirling around her with each breath.

A cough rumbled from her dry throat. A yellow spot appeared next to her. Her hands flew towards it, clenching on anything that offered support. She hit the rough surface, and it jumped back, enlarging the yellow circle. Natalie could see the outline of the flashlight. Cutting her hands, she threw away layers of rubble until the released whole object enveloped her with light that blinded her eyes like the sun on a summer day.

- Thank you, Ethan - she said.

She shined the light on the pile of rubble, revealing a black shape on the moss beside it.

She walked over, groaned, and picked up her backpack.
She stretched out on the green floor. Under the tears in the pants material, red lines and brown bruises covered her skin. She sat there with her hands buried in the moss, which muffled the twitching of her fingers. She pulled out the hip flask, gasping. Her teeth clicked against the metal as she unscrewed the cap.

Her fingers curled like claws and gripped the container as if numb. A spicy scent topped with a nutty note hit her senses. Natalie, still gasping, tipped her hip flask, and a thin stream covered her hand. When she screamed, a small piece of something gray rolled down from the rubble. Natalie took a sip but choked, spilling liquor over her other hand. She held off another scream by biting her lip.

Natalie's head rested on the bulge of her backpack, and she closed her eyes. "I can't do it. I can't", she thought. The drops were hitting louder now. Natalie had the feeling of a sound coming from somewhere above her. Plop. Plop. She sank into them.

Natalie's eyes flicked open, her body aching less than expected. She angled the flashlight to brighten her backpack.
Her hands trembled as they grasped the crinkling foil, revealing bandages and plasters. She wrapped her hands and gasped when the white cloth touched her skin. Just as she was digging deeper into her pack, the sound of glass clinking broke the silence. Her eyebrows shot up, and her mouth fell open.

"Bottle," she thought. Her mind flashed through past moments but couldn't pinpoint when she'd tucked the whiskey bottle into her backpack. Natalie marveled at the bottle's survival from the fall as her head buzzed. The cork squeaked as she pulled it out, a bouquet of alcoholic aromas spread around. She poured the whiskey into her hip flask, then nestled the bottle in her backpack as if she were putting a baby to sleep.

Natalie took a swig from the hip flask, the whiskey warming her throat.

- I guess it's time to find out where this hole goes - she said, her voice bouncing off the infected walls.

The corridor stretched out before her, punctuated by a set of doors—two on each side. The grotesque growths hadn't claimed them as if frequent use kept the invasion at bay. She ventured further, the clatter of her shoes filling the air. No moss muffled her footsteps here. She approached the nearest door, but a dried red mark caught her attention.

The blood strip divided the dirty floor in the middle and disappeared into the distance. Natalie stared at the red streak, immobilized by the weight of the discovery. Spasms of vomiting forced their way into her throat, and impending doom engulfed her as suffocating as a pyroclastic cloud. The crimson of the sickening streak still held her captive, preventing her from moving. Her hand felt heavy as if made of lead, but she lifted it and illuminated the streak more. "Daniel's blood?" she thought.

She came here for him, to help him if he needed it. What she was looking at now was too violent and real. Her head was spinning, and multi-colored reflections were flashing before her eyes. "Run away, run away" she thought.

The outside world seemed to call to her as she remembered what she had left there. Her life. Work. Her passion. She closed her eyes and saw the easel where she often sat. Rows of brushes and paint tubes lined up, waiting for her to use them. She missed the everyday problems, like the long lines at the store or the picky customers who ordered her paintings. They complained that the princess's blonde hair was not blonde enough or that the magic house was too magical.

A sour taste spread across her tongue. Her thoughts were racing, filling her with visions, memories, and scenarios of what could happen here, under the mansion. She turned around and fell to her knees, vomiting. The rapid breathing and tremors racking her entire body made it difficult to get up. And then she heard it.
As quiet as an insect buzzing, she could hear the sound of footsteps somewhere deep inside. Their uneven and slow rhythm reminded Natalie of someone who didn't know where to go. "Daniel?"
The thought crossed her mind, but her voice lodged in her throat. Her eyes locked onto the blood trail. "What if it's not him?"
Her ears strained for footsteps. "What if he's hurt, bleeding out somewhere in this darkness?" Before another thought could form, she found herself sprinting. A shaky flashlight beam darted over the infested walls and the floor. The trail of blood led her like a silent guide. Daniel, bleeding and abandoned, flashed before her. The trail disappeared, but her legs carried her on. She turned left. She ran straight, turned again, and again. Natalie's leg caught on something, and her hands hit the floor with a muffled thud.

The knee stung from the impact. She stood up, rubbing the sore spot. A wooden log lay in the middle of the passage. The air grew thick and cloying, as if something had died in the corner and was now spreading its decay. Each breath brought a heavy, sour tang reminiscent of forgotten meat left out in the summer sun.
The scent clawed at the nostrils, demanding attention like the relentless push of an encroaching tide. The quiet shuffling of feet came from behind her.

A shiver ran down her spine as the sound grew louder, getting closer and closer. "If it were Daniel, he would have recognized me by now," she thought, struggling with her muscles to turn around. A groan, deformed by the echo, reached towards her like hands twisted by disease.

-D...Daniel? - she said without turning around.
The stench became stronger, and she felt dizzy. Another groan echoed behind her, drilling straight into her skull.

She started to run.

The flashing light left painful afterimages in front of her eyes. Her whole body protested, but she kept running. She hit a wall covered with growths. Panting, she inhaled air into her lungs, burning with effort. The stone floor, filthy and full of debris, seemed tempting now. She sat down and stretched her legs. Natalie's hand pressed against her chest, the lingering groan still reverberating in her mind. "That couldn't have been Daniel," she assured herself. "But what the hell is going on here?"
She uncapped her hip flask and took two long swigs.

She had no clue where she'd ended up or how far she'd strayed from where she fell. Casting the flashlight down, she noticed her footprints imprinted on the dusty, sandy floor.
"I could backtrack," the thought flickered in her mind.
She dismissed it, not eager to cross paths with whoever—or whatever—she'd heard earlier. So, she pressed on, deeper into the corridor. The walls around her still bore grotesque biological abominations, a wild, uncontrolled growth reaching every direction.

After some time, she saw small gray shapes on the floor before her, resembling a strange carpet. Rats. Their desiccated bodies contorted into agonizing shapes, limbs indistinguishable from heads. Sunken cavities where their stomachs and eyes should be made her recoil, her hand flying to her mouth. Compassion swelled in her, but fear over what could have done this to them dwarfed that sentiment.
- I'm sorry - she said.
Her footsteps broke their fragile, mummified forms with a sickening crunch. Each snap intensified the squeeze in her stomach.
- I'm sorry - she whispered, tears blurring her vision.
The tiny bodies shattered like glass under her boots. She came upon an ajar wooden door. Pressing her ear against it, she listened. Nothing. Natalie pushed it open to reveal stairs leading downward. Spotting a dark shape on a distant step, she descended and found herself staring at Daniel's camera.

She snatched it up in a reflexive movement. The lens was shattered. The display was busted. She remembered the day Daniel had brought this home, the joy it had sparked in him. "Apart from skill and expertise, that's another thing that separates hobbyists from pros," he had said then. Now, staring at the broken piece of technology, a terrible conclusion settled in her mind.

Daniel might be gone.

Speculation felt useless, theories irrelevant. Reality had just slapped her in the face with the most compelling evidence short of finding Daniel's lifeless body. "But what happened to him?" She shook her head. "No. This means I'm close, and I could still find him. Soon, we will be together again," she thought. Tucking the camera into her backpack, she took two sips from her hip flask. Along with the alcohol, she was filled with the sensation that physical obstacles were not the only danger she might encounter here.

The desire to escape from this hellish abyss grew stronger within her. Something covered the love and care Natalie felt for Daniel. "He may have been dead for several days. And I. I am alive, and I want to live."

While driving here with Ethan, the idea of a life without Daniel had seemed unbearable. Now, the very thought of not surviving at all took center stage. She peered down the stairs.

"What if he's down there, hurt? What if he needs me, and I just run?" Indecision ripped through her, as jolting as lightning splitting a tree. Her eyes darted from the door to the stairs, her flashlight swinging with them.

Then, her gaze rested on the worn wood of the door before she turned and descended the cricking steps.

- Ethan - she whispered.
"Why didn't he come back? He didn't want to come to Gary. It's my fault he ended up here. And if something happened to him because of it, I deserved to die here." The creaking of wood slides into Natalie's stream of thoughts. "I should've listened to Ethan, stayed in Daniel's apartment, and called the cops." She halted, her ears ringing again. Natalie pressed her hand to her ear, feeling the wet stickiness of blood. She examined her fingers, now tinted red in the artificial light. For a moment, she just stared, then licked the thick liquid off her fingers. "Go back inside," the thought.

She'd convinced herself that love and concern fueled her actions. She couldn't just sit by, not knowing Daniel's fate. She needed to see him again. She'd fantasized about finding him asleep in his car, ready to apologize and blame it all on his passion. Then, they'd drive back together, resuming their wonderful life. That notion propelled her at first, but as the struggle wore on, she felt the pull of her own needs. "No," she thought, steeling herself.
"I'd give my life for Daniel." Then, a pause. "But what about Ethan?" She sank onto a step, which groaned and splintered under her. Guilt washed over her for drawing Ethan into another one of her messes. How many times had he bailed her out, forgiven her mistakes? "How could he put up with me for so long?" she wondered. Another voice, still hers but distant and echoing, chimed in.

"Should've thought of that before. Too late for self-pity now."
She drained the rest of the whiskey and hurled the hip flask, which
hit the wall with a metallic clatter.

- Fuck you! - She screamed it out as she stumbled her way down
the stairs.

They led to an archway, and Natalie lit up its interior. Her legs
quivered as she paused. Inside, the smooth stone walls gleamed
and black sand covered the marble floor. She stepped in, boots
crunching over the sandy surface. The room offered no other
exits, just pristine walls devoid of the unsettling growths she'd
seen. "Damn, what now?" she clenched her fists as she looked
around. She'd have to backtrack and traverse the rat graveyard
again. She sat down on the marble floor, legs crossed, sending
plumes of dust swirling around her. She took a bottle from her
backpack, and a twinge flickered across Natalie's face as she
thought of the abandoned hip flask.

"I can go back for her," she thought. The glass surface played with
the light as Natalie tilted the bottle, studying the movement of the
liquid. She breathed in the aroma. Her knee popped as she stood,
drawing a wince from her. Another crack sounded from her spine
as she bent to retrieve the hip flask.

Back in her spot on the marble, she cleaned the hip flask with her sleeve, blowing away the grains of sand.

- I'm sorry, it won't happen again - Natalie said.

- You always say it, and then you do the same - the hip flask said, twisting her lips.

- What? Not true! This was the first time I acted so shamefully, and I am very sorry again - Natalie said.

- The first time was when you and Daniel fought four months ago, right before Krampus Holiday - the hip flask continued in a lecturer's tone. - You threw me at the door as soon as it closed behind him.

- No! I...I don't remember that - Natalie said, her voice trembling.

- Second time. When your mother visited you two months ago, she wanted to talk to you, but you didn't like what she had to say.

- You're lying! - Natalie's voice exploded in the small room.

- The third time was… - the hip flask paused. - I don't remember where it was. Maybe a house party?

- House party? At Lucy's?

- Lucy? Lucy? Is that the redhead? - hip flask said.

- Yes. Sister of Daniel's friend.
The hip flask bared her teeth in a smile.

- Yeah, I remember now! Some guy said that "real painting ended with Caspar D. Friedrich, and everything else after that is shit," and then...

- I threw you right in his ugly face! Yes! I remember that. I'm sorry, but he asked for it.

She moved the hip flask closer to the light.

- Let's see how bad it is. - Natalie said.

- I survive—this time. But promise me, it was the last time.

- Yes! Of course! I promise I will never throw you again... unless it's self-defense. Hip flask sighed.

- Fair enough. Coming back to the point, I hear your throat is dry. Fill me up, baby - the hip flask said, winking at Natalie. Her hands trembled when she filled up the hip flask. The bottle clinked as it returned to a backpack. Natalie took a long swig, then wiped her mouth on her sleeve. "Damn, I'd like to smoke now," she thought.

She furrowed her brow as if rummaging through a mental drawer labeled "Last Cigarette."

- Two years ago? No - she said, staring at the darkness of the ceiling.

- Then I smoked for two more weeks. Yes. I haven't smoked for about a year now.

A short man dressed in a crimson livery trimmed with gold threads whose buttons sparkled like diamonds stepped into the tight circle of light.

- My Lady. Did you call? - the butler said.

- I? No.

- I thought you wanted to smoke, so I brought cigarettes - the butler said.

He handed her a shiny silver tray with a package on it.

- Your favorite, My Lady. Menthol "Leechridden's" in a soft package - he said, bowing his head.

- Oh, yeah! I used to smoke only these. Thank you... - Natalie looked at the man.

- Benson, My Lady.

- Oh, I'm sorry. I keep forgetting - she said, blushing.

- Thank you, Benson.

- My Lady - Benson bowed his head again.

Natalie kneaded the package, which rustled in her fingers.

- It's a pity that the "Leechridden's," like you, are imo... imma... that you are halu... hallucs... illusions. Three lines appeared on Benson's forehead, but the rest of his face remained impassive, like a stone bust of a long-forgotten president.

- Yes, My Lady. I'm hallucination, but "Leechridden's" are very real.

- Can not be! - she said.

The package fell out of her hands. She picked it up. Light danced on the foil.

- Please check, My Lady. I would never lie to you.

The foil rustled, crackling and squeaking as Natalie tugged at the wrapping. She took out a cigarette and turned it over, hearing the creaking of the rolled paper. She smelled it, and the flood of memories hit her like a mudslide. Her mom discovering a 15-year-old her puffing away, the guilt on both faces. Then, the unique taste of Leechridden's filled her senses, and Ethan's encouraging smile as he cheered on her final attempt to quit.

- Would you like fire, My Lady? - Benson asked.

Her large eyes stared at him.

- What?

- Would you like fire, My Lady? - Benson repeated.

- Oh, no... I have my... lighter.

As she finished her sentence, she felt a cold, golden "ZIPPO" in her hand.

The mirror-clear surface of the small rectangle gleamed.

- Benson? - Natalie said.

- Yes, My Lady?

- Can you tell me where I got it?

She raised the shiny object towards the man.

- Yes, My Lady, I can.

The silence stretched, palpable and heavy. Natalie's eyes narrowed, her gaze piercing as she looked at Benson. Butler shifted, the weight of her stare pressed down on him. He swallowed hard, glancing at his outstretched tray, then back to her.

- Can you tell me?

- Do you want me to say it now, My Lady?

- Yes, Benson. Now!

Benson flinched at the raised volume, his eyes darting to meet h ers. His posture straightened.

- Of course, My Lady. Would you mind repeating the question?

She rolled her eyes, sighing.

- Is the lighter I'm holding in my hand real, or is it a hallucination?

- Yes - Benson said.

Natalie's face turned red.

- Which "Yes"? - she said, waving the object in his face.

- It's real. You bought it along with cigarettes and whiskey.
- What? Impossible - her voice trembled.
She stared at the lighter.

Natalie remembered the cold, metal door handle as she entered.
The muted chime of the bell announced her presence.
The fluorescent lights buzzed overhead, casting a stark glow over
the rows of liquor bottles and refrigerated cases.
The faded linoleum underfoot had seen better days, worn down
by hundreds of shoes. Aisle after aisle of colorful bottles greeted
her, their labels promising warmth and escape. At the counter,
her eyes wandered to the cigarettes displayed behind the glass
partition and, next to them, the array of lighters.
"Pack of these," she pointed to her preferred brand of cigarettes.
And without much thought, she added, "And that lighter.
The cashier, a young man with tattoos snaking up his arms,
had nodded, placing her chosen items on the counter. With a swift
movement, he grabbed a bottle of whiskey, tilting it so she could
see the label.
- Single malt "Tekeli-li" like always? - he asked.
- Sure - Natalie said.
Money exchanged hands, and the cashier packed her purchases
into a paper bag, the bottle's weight making the bag stretch and sag.

- I...I did buy it. I remember now - Natalie said.
The tray in the butler's hand trembled and began to bend as if it
were melting.

The shimmer from the polished silver caught the glint of the lighter as Natalie tilted it in her hand. Benson's cold, unyielding demeanor contrasted with the confusing whirl of her own emotions. He straightens the tray and wipes it with a cloth.

- So I'm really holding a lighter and cigarettes?

- Yes, My Lady.

She bit her lip, frowning.

- All right. In that case, I'll smoke it now.

- Of course, My Lady.

There were a few coughs, a cloud of smoke rising in front of her. She watches it until swirling, transparent vapor fades, then takes another puff. A few beads of sweat roll down Benson's face, glistening and disappeared under a white shirt collar.

-Benson?

-Yes, My Lady?

- Are you sweating? - she said.

- Please forgive me, but unfortunately, yes.

- But why if you're not real?

- Please forgive me, My Lady, but I don't know the answer this time. Natalie flicked away the ash accumulating on her cigarette.

- Oh, okay. Don't worry - she said and took a puff. - Benson?

- Yes, My Lady?

- Is Benson your name or surname?

- Surname, My Lady - he said.

- Oh, and what's your name?

- Butler, My Lady.

- Butler Benson?

Benson nodded. - Can I serve you anything else, My Lady? If not, I have to return to the kitchen and ensure the cook doesn't eat the gardener again.

- Please wait. I have one more question.

- Yes, My Lady?

- Do You know where Daniel is?

- I'm very sorry, but I don't know the current whereabouts of Master Daniel. However, can I make a suggestion? - he said.

- Yes, of course, Benson. I have always taken your opinions into account.

- Thank you, My Lady, it means a lot to me. I wanted to tell you to pay attention to the surroundings. This room might not be real. Natalie braced her hands on the floor, and the cigarette landed on the marble with a quiet hiss.

- What? How so? So where am I? - she asked.

- Well, I'm not sure, My Lady, but it's possible that you're still sitting on the steps in front of the entrance.
Natalie started to stand up, pursing her lips. Benson held out his hand to her, and she leaned on it.

- Thank you, Benson.

- At your service, My Lady. Can I make one more suggestion?

- Yes, please. Speak boldly. Your advice and suggestions have always supported our multi-generational family, even in the times of Emperor Franz Joseph I.

- Thank you, My Lady, you are too kind. I wanted to say that smoking is harmful to your health.

On the packaging, you will find a hotline number whose consultants will help you overcome this very disastrous addiction. And please don't lose your lighter. It will come in handy when the batteries run out.

- Batteries? - she said.

- You're welcome, My Lady. Now, if you'll excuse me, the cook is calling me. It seems that he ate the gardener...again. If you need me, My Lady, please just ring the bell.

The butler retreated, disappearing into the darkness. Natalie stared at the void he had just filled. "Damn, I didn't ask Benson about our cook's name," she thought.

Chapter Six.

Natalie's fingers grazed the cold stairs, memories of the butler's sudden appearance fresh in her mind. She took another cautious step downward. Before her stood a door, its faded wooden panels framed by crumbling stone. The grain of the weathered wood caught the dim light, punctuated by rustic metal studs and dark iron brackets. Beyond, the echo of dripping water played a soft rhythm. Plop. Plop. Plop.

Natalie shook her head and rubbed her neck. Gritting her teeth, she pressed against the door, which creaked as it moved. She felt sweat trickle down her back as her face and hands pressed against the wooden surface.

As the door creaked open, a corridor revealed itself. The walls, stained and mottled with age, bore a decay pattern while an intricate design of faded burgundy swirled underfoot. Wooden doors weathered just like the entrance lined the hallway, their surfaces marred by years of neglect. Thick and heavy air filled her. A pang of unease settled in her stomach. She paused, listening to the far dripping interrupted only by her heartbeat. At the far end, shadows hinted at another passage. With each step, the beam from her flashlight jumped from one door to the next, revealing brass handles tarnished with age.

The cold metal resisted her, none yielding to her pull.

- Daniel! Daniel! - her voice echoed, bouncing off the corridor's walls. Hands shaking, she pulled at each handle, but each one remained unmoved. She approached the stairs. The tarnished metal steps groaned under her weight, each bearing the scars and blemishes of rust as if the metal itself were decaying beneath her.

Each creak and groan from the staircase sounded like the building's own sinister lullaby, luring her further up into the darkness. Reaching the top of the stairs, Natalie's gaze locked onto the door ahead.

Its once vibrant hue had long since been eroded, revealing layers of rust and chipped paint that bore the harsh passage of time. Turquoise patina accents contrasted with the dark rust, creating a map of wear and corrosion. The crooked and aged latch seemed as if it might crumble with a mere touch. Every creak of the stairs beneath her seemed to echo back from the door as if beckoning her closer. When she reached it, she hesitated for just a moment. Her fingers brushed over the rough, rusted surface. Taking a deep breath, she gripped the latch, its cold bite piercing her fingers, and pushed the door open with a haunting, grating sound.

Another corridor spread beyond the door, its end swallowed by an impenetrable darkness. "I know this place," Natalie thought. Visions of her younger self bubbled up. She remembered the hotel corridor where she and her parents stayed during the holiday season. A bright red carpet decorated with a gold geometric pattern, walls in warm shades of yellow separated by rectangles of smooth brown doors.

Above, a white ceiling from which cool halogen light streamed down onto her. A hideous and devastated copy of that place stretched before her. The worn carpet, black with soot and dirt, was also covered with small pieces of waste, feces, and animal bones. Everything crunched under her feet, sand, glass, stones, and small bones. Natalie noticed an oblong skull with fangs. She crouched down next to it. "Is that a dog?" she thought. The peeling paint was falling off the walls, revealing greasy stains on the remains of the plaster and bare bricks in some places.

Each breath forced her to inhale the smell of mustiness, excrement, and decay. The cracked laminate of the door made it look like the skin of an old man. Holes gaped where the door handles were, like the eye sockets of dead cyclops. Patches of mixed colors, browns, yellows, and reds covered the ceiling. Long streaks of cracks emerged from beneath them. She kept walking, covering her mouth and nose with her hand. Her steps varied, adapting to the obstacles beneath her feet. The rows of doors stretched on, never leaving her side. The end of the corridor seemed to recede as if in a dream, refusing to be caught in the embrace of light. There was a metallic clang as her foot nudged something. Light swept across the floor, revealing pebbles, shards of glass, syringes, and pools of something brown. In the midst of it, Natalie spotted a metal object. "Doorknob," she thought and stretched out her hand. The rusty metal left stains on her fingers. Natalie headed for the nearest door.

A shower of brown crumbs fell as she inserted the doorknob into the hole and turned it with a grating sound.

The door creaked open. A squeak escaped her lips as the trembling light revealed the interior.

The shoes are stacked from floor to ceiling, like a mountain of madness waiting to be explored. Shoes of brown and black, with both thick and thin soles, converged into what looked like a macabre piece of installation art. Footwear filled every corner of the small room. Just inside the entrance lay a pair of shoes, blue leather with three white stripes. The thick rubber soles were covered with mud. "What did he wear when he came here?" she thought. She stood staring at the blue sneakers as spasms of vomiting shook her.

Next, she was kneeling on the floor, her chest heaved, each breath ragged, as she fought back the urge to choke. She got up and slammed the door from which a piece of laminate had fallen off. The noise echoed down the corridor.

Natalie passed door after door with no handles, holding her stomach. At the end of the corridor, she saw a door.

The white surface stood out from the damaged wall, shining with freshness. The round door handle shimmered golden, reflecting the light. She sighed, and when she turned the handle with a trembling hand, the door opened, revealing another dark corridor. She walked through the door.

A sudden crash behind her made her heart skip a beat. Natalie dropped the flashlight. She reached for it, and when she stood up, the cold light falling from the snow-white ceiling hit her.

Through squinted eyes, Natalie saw a bright red carpet
decorated with even gold patterns. She felt it under her feet, soft
as if no one had ever walked on it. Brown smooth doors at regular
gaps stretched along the clean walls, the color of which brought to
mind a warm spring day.

- Damn, more delusions - she said.
She heard a rustling of wood as one of the doors opened.
A plump blonde with bangs cut above her eyebrows emerged from
inside, carrying a black plastic bag in both hands. The black foil
was bulging in several places.

Two children walk with her, holding onto her green dress.
"Fuck, not her," Natalie thought. The woman and children were
approaching, appearing as if they were floating above the floor.
Natalie darted for the door, her hand brushing against the smooth
wall. Natalie hit the wall that replaced the door several times with
a dull thud.

When she turned, the blonde woman was there, alone, the plastic
bag oozing a dark red liquid. Natalie backed away until she felt the
cold wall. Thick saliva passed through her tightened throat.

- I know you're not the real Mary, so you can stop this bullshit!

Not-Mary threw the plastic black bag on the floor, and it hit the
floor with a crunch, scattering drops all over the place.
Natalie's eyelids clamped shut, an instinctive shield against the
horror, but the brief glimpse was etched into her brian.
Visceral details—shapes, textures, and colors—lingered behind
her closed eyes, vivid and inescapable.

The gruesome inventory of the bag's contents invaded her thoughts, unbidden and vile, a parade of the macabre that twisted her stomach into knots. She took a deep, shuddering breath, trying to dispel the image, but it clung to her like a shadow. The damp, metallic scent from the opened bag mingled with the air, a silent confirmation of the nightmare that her mind had already pieced together.

A dead Golden Retriever lay on the floor. Its paws were twisted, and its light yellow-white fur was caked with blood.

- And yes, I'm not real, but you really did it! - Not-Mary said, pointing to the dead animal.

Natalie's legs gave way, and she slid down the wall, which creaked from the friction of her backpack.

- It was an accident! I did not see him! - Natalie said.

- You knew you shouldn't drive, and yet...

- Hold on a moment! I didn't run him over. Your... or rather their, dog died peacefully in the apartment. He was about 13 years old.

- All right. You got me. You didn't kill "Brigadier Lethbridge." Not-Mary raised her finger and lowered it with her gaze.

- Look again.

Natalie's looked downwards. The human head looked at her with unseeing eyes. The skin was covered with filth, and the neck was covered with blood.

- But Ethan died because of you! - Not-Mary said.

Natalie looked from the head to the fake Mary.

- Seriously? Head? Maybe you'd better dance the "Macarena," it will be much scarier. Not-Mary brushed something off her green dress and cleared her throat.

- I don't know how to dance it - she said. - I always preferred "Coco Jamboo."

A spasm went through Natalie, and her body rose from the floor. She felt her limbs stiffen. Numb, they felt like they belonged to someone else. Music started playing in the corridor, and dance rhythms filled her head. Natalie's arms lifted and dipped of their own accord, and each movement synced to a rhythm that pulsed through her. The floor vibrated, transmitting an energy that made her knees bend and straighten.

- Nice moves. You should do this more often - Not-Mary said and started dancing with her. Natalie twirled, her limbs moving with grace and ease.

She felt the music in her bones like she had been born to dance. Together, Natalie and Not-Mary's voices filled the hallway, their duet reviving the lyrics of a forgotten summer anthem. "Ayyayaya Coco Jamboo ayyayai ayyayaya Coco Jamboo ayyayai ayye yo."

The music seeped into Natalie's very essence, syncing her heartbeat with the bassline. It was as if the song had rewired her pulse. Door after door swung open, spilling out men and women who joined the spontaneous carnival. Their bodies became instruments of joy. Arms waved, hips gyrated, feet leaped—all in a tapestry of unexpected euphoria. It wasn't a display of precision but a celebration of liberation.

the air with their style and flair. They smiled, laughed, and cheered, letting go of their worries and fears. Arms reached for the heavens in one moment and extended outward in the next as if to embrace the world. The dance floor pulsated with life, an organic evolution of moves.

A conga line snaking through the crowd, side-steps in unison, hands and arms weaved patterns to a rhythm that promised no end. "Ayyayaya Coco Jamboo ayyayai ayyayaya Coco Jamboo ayyayai ayye yo."

***

Natalie knelt on the dirty floor, staring at the light beam stretching before her. She grasped the flashlight. Its beam revealed an empty corridor, the solitude hitting her with sudden clarity. It was once again a dark old place, its walls lined with doors without handles. Her legs shook as she stood, and the pressure she felt caused a scream to escape her lips. "I really danced," she thought as she massaged her calves.

- Hey! Hey! Get over yourself, girl! - hip flask said. Natalie pulled her out.

- You're wandering around this garbage dump, and poor me, I'm lying in this musty backpack.

- I'm sorry - Natalie said and drank from the hip flask.

- OK. Now I have two pieces of news for you, good and bad.

- Yes? Please tell me.

- The good thing is that you didn't dance, and the bad thing is that you actually had a seizure or maybe some muscle spasticity - hip flask said.

Natalie wiped her mouth with the back of her hand, feeling the warmth of the alcohol in her throat.

- What is muscle spasticity?

- I don't know, I'm not a doctor. But you should see a specialist about it, you know... as soon as you get back to that wonderful everyday normality.

- Yes, I'll do that. Thanks for taking care of me. You're the only one who has never let me down - Natalie said.

- Oh, come on, before I'll blush.

Natalie wiped her mouth after taking another sip.

- I mean it. You always said "yes" and stood by me when I needed you.

- Well, that's right - hip flask said, smiling.

Natalie took another sip and stared at the corridor. It split into two ways. The growths covered the wall before her.
They stretched along both
sides, looming at the edge of the light, looking like creatures ready to attack.

- Where should we go?

- Definitely not to the left.

Natalie moved the hip flask closer.

- Why not go left?

- Because you went there earlier and had a blast at the non-existent disco.

- What? I don't remember going that way.

- Honey, are you still surprised by such a thing?

Natalie sighed.

- Right. This place wants to break me, but my sober and logical mind won't allow it. And with your help, hip flask, we will succeed.

- Hell yeah! Keep it up, sister. That's the spirit - hip flask said.

Natalie aimed the flashlight at the right branch, feeling a chill in her spine.

- Let's go then - she said.

At the very end, she saw a door. Similar to the ones she had seen before, wooden and damaged. The hinges creaked as Natalie walked through the door. After a few steps, she stopped, and her heart started pounding again.

The light from her flashlight moved from floor to ceiling, revealing the iron abomination. A large metal table, bed frames, various pieces of sheet metal and shelves, and rolls of mesh stuffed into the gaps. All this stacked together blocked access to the rest of the corridor. She approached with her hand outstretched as if approaching a wild animal. She felt cold, which turned into warmth when she pulled the most protruding element of the structure several times. A metallic creak pierced her ears, but the barricade remained intact.

"That was stupid. The damn thing could have just as collapsed on me," she thought and shuddered. "Could Daniel have built it?" She moved her face towards the obstacle.

-Daniel! Daniel! Daniel!

When no more sounds could come out of her throat, she started listening. Nothing. She stood there for a moment and then sat on the floor, taking off her backpack. She rested the flashlight next to her. Natalie drank from the hip flask and set it down on the floor with a clatter. A package of menthol Leechridden's rustled, and soon slender ribbons of smoke rose upwards, disappearing into the darkness beneath the ceiling.

"What now? Turn back?" she thought as she blew out a cloud of smoke. The smell of cigarette spread throughout the room, mixing with mustiness and an odor that Natalie couldn't recognize. "If this piece of metal garbage is standing between Daniel and me, I can't turn back," she thought. A chill ran down her neck. "But if there's something there that should stay behind the barricade?"

Another shiver shook her spine. "Unless there's a safe zone there, and I'm stuck on the wrong side?" She exhaled smoke, and the cigarette glow flashed red and flew into the tangle of iron.

And then, darkness fell. Natalie felt for the flashlight and flicked the switch a few times.

- NO. NO. NO. - she said.

She shook the object several times, but the light did not return. The overwhelming blackness engulfed everything, leaving no glow, shape, or outline. Her breathing became ragged, and each exhalation was louder than the last. The floor felt colder and colder as if all the warmth had gone with the light.

The tightness in her chest spread and encompassed her chest.

A spasm of sobs escaped Natalie's lips. She felt like darkness was seeping into her, filling her with a growing sense of hopelessness with every passing second. She felt a scream creeping from her trembling throat, and her hands flew to her mouth, pressing it hard. Now that she couldn't see anything, making a sound seemed like a signal to whatever might be roaming the darkness. Even Natalie's heart seemed to be beating too loud. Each subsequent beat in the rhythm of terror turned seconds into hours. Despite the cold cocooning around her, she sank to the floor and closed her eyes.

***

Natalie looked at the blue tiled wall, her feet resting on the cotton rug. Drops fell one by one from the shiny tap. She looked around—a white cabinet with a mirror hanging above the washbasin and a shower cabin on the right. "Bathroom again," she thought. She looked at her reflection.

Her skin was clean, without any wounds or dried blood. She ran her hand through her hair, feeling how soft and fresh it was. The scent of larch reached her nostrils, its subtle aroma filling the bathroom. "I'm going to stand here and enjoy this view. Especially since I'll probably never see it again," she thought. She looked at all the elements and compared them with the remembered details.

"The nightmare will get me anyway. My eyes will probably fall out soon, the walls will start to rot, or something will drag me into the drain." Still, the room remained immaculate, every surface shining, untouched, as if part of a showroom display.

A soft knock on the door broke her contemplation.

- Hey, are you okay? - the voice reached through the door, its concern slicing through the calm facade of the bathroom.
The sound of voice shook her, making it impossible to react. Millions of needles pierced her mind. "I need to hear it again, and I'll be sure," she thought.

- Natalie? We are starting to worry.

- Daniel? - she said.

- Are you okay? - Daniel said in a low voice.
She stared at the door as if trying to see through it.

- Y...yes. Yes - she said, feeling tears flowing down her cheeks.

- Yes, I'm okay. Cold water ran down her trembling hands as she rinsed her face. Ran down her eyelids and trembling lips. She heard conversations over the hum of ventilation and closed doors.

Natalie left the bathroom and entered the room, lit by daylight streaming through the large glass doors of the balcony. Friendly glances greeted her, and her eyes darted from one face to the next. Her relatives sat at a rectangular table covered with food and drinks. A cake studded with candles stood in the center of the table. The number 40, placed in the center of the cake, flowed to her from a whole stream of smells and sensations. A petite woman with gray hair who looked like a much older version of Natalie stood up from the table.

- You're so pale. Are you okay? - woman asked.

- I'm fine, mom. It's probably just tiredness - Natalie said.

- Come, sit with us - woman said.

She felt a hand on her side, Daniel leading her to the table. With his other hand, he pointed to a chair for her. Natalie stared at him. His serene brown eyes looked back at her. He pulled a chair for her, and Natalie sat down. Everyone was sitting at the table, although the children fidgeted and asked Mary to let them play outside.

- You'll be leaving in a moment, my larks. First, your aunt will blow out the candles - Mary said. Natalie got up and blew out the candles.

The cake with the 40 sticking out of the middle caught her eye again, obscuring everything else on the table with its creamy chocolate bulk. Dripping with chocolate and cream, it seemed so heavy that it was about to crush the table, piercing the floors of other apartments all the way to the basement and beyond.

A flash broke her from this sensation, and a silver triangle emerged before her. The cake spatula landed in her hand, and Daniel spoke right next to her ear.

- Please do the honors.

The warmth of Daniel's fingers spread across her hand, and the fingers of the other pressed harder into Natalie's side.

The cake was closer now, the aroma of chocolate and cocoa licking its way into the nasal cavity, seeping into the nerve bundles and splashing across the nerve bulbs. Natalie sees more shades and colors in the brown icing, which has a wavy, lumpy texture. Thick and gliding down like a snail, it shone with shades of brown that looked like khaki and sprinkled with chaotic yellow spots.

- I'll help you, honey - Daniel said.

Natalie felt her hand approach the cake, the triangular blade digging into the muddy, thin lumps that fell to the table with a splash. The downward movement causes yellow-white goo to flow from inside, sticking to the spatula's blade. This time, Natalie smelled the eggs mixed with boiled cabbage left in the sun.

- Take a plate - Daniel said.

There was a clink of china, and Natalie saw a white plate with a floral pattern in front of her.

- Please, take a piece. You, my dear, deserve the biggest - he said, not letting go of her. Natalie's hand was guided by Daniel as if some illness had deprived her of the ability to feed herself. Spongy lumps fell off the melting goo, dripping from the plate and splashing the table.

Natalie felt pressure on her head and chin and then noticed Mary.

- Don't worry, it's just a birthday hat - she said.

The children ran up with their fingers outstretched.

- Ha, ha, what a stupid hat!

- Ha, ha, as stupid as the aunt who wears it!

Mary hugs the children.

- My larks, it's not nice to laugh at sick people - she said, grinning. Natalie felt fingers digging into her side.

- Why did you put so little on your plate, honey? It's your birthday. You have to eat more than everyone else - he said.

- Exactly - Mary added and stuck her hand into the cake, which emitted an intermittent hiss of air accompanied by wet splatters resembling gases rising under the surface of a swamp.

Mary reached out with her hand full of dripping goo and dropped it onto the plate, then wiped herself on Natalie's t-shirt.

- I'm afraid this will leave a stain - Mary said.

Mary, the children, and Daniel all burst into laughter that tears the mind like hooks. Natalie looks around the room. Her mother and Ethan stand behind the closed balcony door, their backs moving as they talk. Daniel's fingers dig into her side again.

- You know what, honey? A spoon won't do. Here, use this.

He put the straw into her mouth, and Mary pressed the back of her head.

- Happy Birthday - they say at the same time.

The tip of the straw disappeared into the ooze, the stench of which hit the nostrils even stronger.

- Slurp! Slurp! Slurp! - the children shout.

- Slurp! Slurp! Slurp! - Mary shouts.

- Slurp! Slurp! Slurp! - Daniel shouts.

Natalie sucked on the stinking goo, hearing herself slurping. She felt the warm contents approaching her mouth. The goo spread on the tongue, spongy lumps sticking to the palate. Cake slime filled her mouth.

Chapter Seven.

The fog receded, giving way to the creeping dusk. The swaying wild grasses added a bit of movement to the otherwise static place. The chirping of crickets wove a comforting melody through the air, a gentle lullaby for any wandering soul. Thin branches of low bushes grew from the ground like skeletal hands trying to grab those who would dare to tread this way. One tree stood out from the rest of the landscape.

A leafless giant stands against the twilight, its branches reaching toward the sky in a tangle of wooden tendrils. Sunlight cast a honeyed glow over the scene, softening the twilight's embrace. Each twisted limb bore the rugged marks of time and illness, their contortions a silent chronicle of survival. The gnarled and rough trunk bears the scars of age, missing chunks of bark that reveal the raw, beaten wood within. The tree holds its ground in this sparse landscape, like a castaway on a deserted island.

A lonely ant wandered through the tall grass. She didn't stop for a moment, pushing forward in a direction only she knew.
She began climbing the wrinkled bark once she reached the tree's roots. The bark curled and folded over itself, etching deep grooves into the tree's skin.

Years carved lines and troughs into the surface, weaving a tapestry of ridges that bore the tree's history. Sun and wind had hardened the outer layer into a labyrinth of wrinkles. Ant's nimble legs led her higher and higher over the bumps and curves.
She reached the most extended branch and stopped at its bent end, swaying in the gusts of wind. The ant dug its mandibles into the hard material and froze again, moved only by a few vibrations passing through her body.

The thuds of bulky boots, mingling with the creak of strained fabric and the clang of metal, echoed across the grassy expanse.
- These could be pantries - Fintifluch said. - In the past, storing food in the ground was normal.
- Some kind of natural refrigerators? - Maya said.
- Hmm...yeah, I guess we can call it that. Barrels or other types of containers with food were buried in the holes, and when the right moment came, the family gathered and dug out the supplies.
- Clever. Although it seems risky. Sure, they are deep enough to prevent animals from getting to them, but what about other people?
For example, neighbors who prefer the easy way? - she said.

Maya looked at him, raising an eyebrow. Fintifluch adjusted one of the straps slung over his shoulder.

- Of course, this solution was far from perfect, but I suspect it was somehow managed. Probably with the help of man's best friend and man's other best friend...the shotgun.

A playful twinkle lit up Maya's eyes, the corners of her mouth twitching upwards in an almost imperceptible smile. She stopped to adjust the leather case on her belt before continuing.

- Given how far the mansion is from other buildings, I don't think they had any problems with it. We should remember that in the past, there were even fewer of them here.
The only question left is...

- Fin. - Maya interrupted him. - We're here

A gaping black hole yawned open a few meters ahead, its maw wide enough that Fintifluch could have sunk into its grab.
They moved forward, each step echoing with a metallic clink as their gear jostled and rattled against each other. They stopped just above the edge of a deep hole. Maya gave a prolonged, low whistle, her gaze lingering on the abyssal void before them.

- It's something new - Fintifluch said.
The hole was lined with sheet metal, the vast sheets of which were adjacent to each other, overlapping one another. Despite the dents, the rusty metal sheet separated the ground from the hole.
Fintifluch paused, his eyes drawn downward by the shadowy depths beneath them. Then, he saw a wooden ladder near his feet.

Fintifluch crouched down, and the ladder trembled and creaked under the pressure of his hands. Then he checked the first few rungs, which creaked but did not bend. He stood up, dusting off his hands.

- It looks solid - he said.
Maya shook her head.

- Before we decide to go down there, we need to do a more thorough inspection - she said.

- Of course, my dear - he said, taking off his backpack, which rattled in several places. He extracted a few thin green tubes from it and then broke them. A poisonous green glow bathed Fintifluch and then illuminated the hole. The green light bounced off the sheet metal in hundreds of distorted reflections until its journey stopped. Through the green glow that filled the opening, Maya and Fintifluch saw the earthy ground as smooth as a tomb's slab. Maya took off her backpack and crouched down.

- Not as deep as before - she said.
The stones crunched as he crouched down next to her.

- About four meters - he said, rubbing his forehead.

- All right. I'm coming down!

- Let's get you ready then.
Fintifluch fastened the clasps on his helmet, and each one emitted a satisfying click as it locked into place. Near his mouth was a curved protruded microphone tube. Maya ran her fingers over the helmet's surface, feeling the familiar contours of the oblong flashlight on the right and the camera at its center. Her touch was meticulous, ensuring everything was in place.

He handed Maya a device, flat and sleek like a smartphone but distinct, with two thick antennas jutting out from its edges. Maya tapped the screen a few times and gave him a thumbs up.

- Vision's fine. Let's check the sound - she said.

Fintifluch cleared his throat, his voice adopting a dramatic flair.

- "In the greenest of our valleys
By good angels tenanted,
Once a fair and stately palace—
Radiant palace—reared its head.
In the monarch Thought's dominion,
It stood there!
Never seraph spread a pinion
Over fabric half so fair!" - he smiled when he finished.

A smirk played on Maya's lips.

- A simple "microphone test" would suffice. But yes, everything's working perfectly.

With a swift, practiced motion, Fintifluch reached into his leather holster and withdrew a black object. The pistol boasted a polymer frame, its grip etched with a stippled pattern to ensure a firm grasp. Its ergonomic design cradled the shooter's hand, the backstrap's gentle curve merging into an integrated beavertail for a superior hold. Matching the frame, the slide presented in matte black, its rear adorned with serrations to offer a steadfast grip during operation. The slide's crest remained unadorned save for the "10mm AUTO" marking etched upon it.

The serial number appeared close to the slide's end, with "NEWINGTON, NH USA" inscribing the weapon's birthplace. An accessory rail positioned ahead of the trigger guard awaited the addition of tactical enhancements like lights or lasers.
A practiced hand glided over the cool metal, familiarity in every motion. Fintifluch ejected the magazine with a swift flick, eyeing the gleaming 10mm rounds nestled within. He nodded at the sight, then returned the magazine to its home with a satisfying click.

His following motion was to rack the slide, peering into the chamber. Noting the absence of a round, he honored the cardinal rule of safety. With a swift release, the slide snapped into place, chambering a round with the crisp sound of readiness.
Fintifluch thumb swept over the safety, ensuring it was off, before his grip firmed, index finger resting along the side of the frame, away from the trigger. A quiet click of the latch confirmed the gun was returned to its holster.

- Fin, really? It's just a hole - Maya said.
- You know what they say, "Stay strapped or get clapped."

She kissed him on the cheek, then broke other green tubes and attached them to his wrists and ankles. Fintifluch descends on the ladder, the faint creaking of the rungs following him down. He felt the texture of the wood under his fingers, porous and rough. Tiny marks on his skin disappeared after a second. There was a soft thump as his feet landed on the glowing green hardened soil. The smell of moist earth reached him first, then something irritating his nostrils flowed from somewhere below.

Maya looked down after him, glancing at the display from time to time. Strands of her hair fluttered free from the tight bun. She tucked a few behind her ear and adjusted the small earpiece with a microphone. Fintifluch walked to one of the rounded walls and crouched, his movements sending a rustle of earth echoing in Maya's earpiece. On the screen, she saw a dark rectangle close to the ground. It reminded her of a cat door.

With a quick movement, she brushed a few strands of hair from her forehead.

- Hey, is this hole in the hole? - she said.

A crackle in her ear preceded Fintifluch's voice, an echo resounding from her earpiece and the hole's depths.

- Affirmative. Wait, let me get some better lighting.

She looked down as Fintifluch pulled something from one of his many pockets, her eyes returning to the screen. The rectangular opening flooded with white light, revealing a long tunnel that gleamed metallic.

- Do you have a good vision, my dear? - he asked.

Maya nodded, a smile spreading across her face.

- Yes. I see a damn long, tight tunnel - she said.

There were several grating sounds from below, ending with a metallic echo.

- It might be a drain of sorts.

He knocked on one of the walls again, and the metallic grating sound echoed through Maya's earpiece.

- It's lined with sturdier metal than what's over me. Can you see the floor? - Fintifluch said.

Maya stared at the display, which showed pebbles, leaves, the scattered bones of a small animal, gray mud, and the outlines of sticks in the harsh light.

- Yes. A lot of crap from the area.

As the buzzing and crackling of the earpiece intensified, Maya looked down to see Fintifluch ascending the ladder. She removed the earpiece and rubbed her ear. When he reached the top, she extended her hand, pulling him up with a firm grip, and then he stood next to her.

He removed his helmet, which rattled with straps and fasteners, and continued the conversation.

- Precisely. That would mean it's not...

- A natural refrigerator - Maya said.

- Yeah, that's one thing. And the second thing. Where does all this water go?

- Could it have been used to irrigate the soil?

Fintifluch ran his fingers through his hair, and Maya smoothed it a few times.

- I don't think so, but it would be best to check what's hidden in this tunnel. Maya clapped with a grin, revealing her white teeth.

- I can try to squeeze in there. I haven't had an opportunity like this since Melon Heads.

Maya clasped her hands together, bouncing on her feet with childlike impatience. Fintifluch smiled, placed his hands on her shoulders, and leaned down to plant a tender kiss on her forehead.

- You know how much I love your courage and willingness to explore, but we will need help here. Prepare Caderouss, my dear.

Maya clapped her hands again.

- Yes, sir! - she said, snapping a playful salute. - It's time for my baby to stretch those metal bones!

Maya placed a big metal suitcase on the ground, its smooth surface gleaming in the evening light. She then entered a multi-digit code on the tiny keyboard's squeaky buttons on the suitcase's side. Something inside beeped, and two thick tabs on the handle lifted with a hiss. She opened it.

- Did you miss me, Caderouss? Because I missed you very much. Now we'll get you ready and go for a walk - she said, manipulating her hands inside.

Maya was holding a curved object with round buttons, knobs, a speaker in the middle, and a small screen sticking out of the top. She pressed buttons and fiddled with knobs, her tongue lolling out in thought. Fintifluch looked over her shoulder.

- Are we good?

Maya looked at him like a child who got his dream toy.

- Yes. I finished entering the parameters and made a few minor updates. She stepped forward, shaking a
few strands of hair from her forehead.

- Now, let's do a warm-up.

A robust robot stood anchored on its caterpillar tracks. The silver of the metal body gleamed in the small reflector's light. Mounted on its mobile base, a mechanical arm stretched out, its articulated joints promising grace and power in every movement.

The quiet hum of the servo motors matched the melody of the cicadas. The arm ended in a versatile and precise claw, capable of disarming danger as it handled the delicate intricacies of manipulation. Like mechanical veins, wires cascaded from its steel frame, suggesting a labyrinth of circuitry beneath the surface. Cameras perched on a rotating axis scanned the environment, missing nothing with their unblinking lenses. In this machine, precision and strength found their embodiment.

- I love watching how much joy you get from playing with your toys - Fintifluch said and kissed her.

The metal walls magnified the light and mechanical grinding that filled the tunnel. Caderouss pushed forward, making the caterpillar tracks glide along with regular grunts. The constant humming and grating faded with each passing moment, leaving only the blurred echo of the robot's travels in Fintifluch's ears. He made his way to the ladder and ascended to rejoin his wife. Maya sat cross-legged on a rubber-like thick green mat.

A vertical rectangle illuminated her face, her eyes staring at the small screen as if there was nothing beyond it. Her fingers seemed to be living beings that manipulated the knobs and pressed buttons. The faint grating noise from the device was similar to what Fintifluch had heard in the tunnel. The squeak of his shoes reached her ears, but her eyes remained on the screen. He sat down next to her on a free piece of mat and stretched out his legs.

- How's he doing?

He looked at her face, covered with flashes from the display.
Maya didn't seem to hear him as she continued steering.
   - He's still wading through this tunnel. This damn thing seems
endless - Maya said.
Fintifluch moved closer, resting his chin on her shoulder. His eyes
shifted toward the display, and he felt a chill wind on his head.

Caderouss glided through the monotony of the unchanging
tunnel, always ahead. The bright light sharpened the outlines of
the metal walls, causing Fintifluch to squint his eyes. Caderouss
lit up an opening before him, a tiny notch that crowned the tunnel.
The tracks squeaked as they stopped in front of him. He paused,
scanning the opening with his camera eye. Something inside the
robot hums, and its upper part begins to lower. The gripper arm
and the upper piece with the camera almost touched the base.
   Caderouss emitted sharp, metallic buzzes, the sound slicing
through the tunnel. The camera image bounced and shook, and
the clatter of metal filled the large circular room. Caderouss rode
on a grid beneath which lay greenish, thickened water.

   Outside, Maya and Fintifluch sighed in unison, staring at the
screen. Maya looked at her husband.
   - Well, now we know where all the water goes - she said.
Fintifluch rubbed his eyes, then moved closer to the display,
touching Maya's face with his cheek.
   - Incredible! What a great project - he said.
Maya looked at him, raising an eyebrow.

- Yes, Fin, great. Now, please explain why it's so great?

- Sorry, my dear, I'll explain. I've seen solutions like this before, and you were half right. This is an irrigation system but not for soil.

Maya rubbed her neck, staring at Fintifluch. The melodies of cicadas filled the space around them, and Maya nudged his shoulder.

- Fin.

Fintifluch looked away from the display and met his wife's gaze.

- Sorry. If this structure is similar to those I know, there are several holes at the bottom of the tank through which water enters other parts of the complex.

- Okay, that's actually pretty cool, but what hydrates?

- Unfortunately, I cannot say that, my dear.

The mat creaked as Fintifluch stood up, and Maya followed him with her eyes.

- I assume that the water is distributed through a network of connections traveling beneath us. However, I am sure the answer to this question will be found under the mansion.

Maya stretched her legs and started to stand up when Fintifluch gave her a hand to lean on.

- Maybe they bred a specimen like the Lake Michigan Monster or the Globster.

- Yes, I thought about that too. - Let's see if Caderouss finds anything else.

Maya returned to the controller, and the display light illuminated her face again.

Caderouss slid along the grate, the irregularities of which shook the camera image. At the end of the room, they noticed a hole identical to the one through which the robot entered.
The light revealed another narrow, metal-walled tunnel as he approached the hole.

- And I was already afraid that nothing else would be here
- Maya said, her fingers tapping on the controller.

Caderouss entered the tunnel, humming and grinding.
The metal, covered with yellow-brown residue, vibrated under the machine's pressure as it pushed forward, illuminating the darkness of the unknown.

Chapter Eight.

A rhythmic sound made its way into Natalie's consciousness in the darkness. Plop. Plop. Plop.

The rhythm drew her from the depths of her nightmare into her waking nightmare. She felt angular shapes pressing into her backpack, the pain permeating her entire body. Natalie opened her eyes and thought of a lighter in her pocket. There was a clang, and the orange flame began to ripple, spreading a warm glow around her.

She was sitting on a pile of rubble, a collection of bricks, boards, bars, and the remains of various junk. Above her was a jagged remnant of the floor, spread out like the toothless mouth of a sea creature, swallowing everything that fell into it. Natalie stared at the ruined floor above her.

"I'm at the broken trapdoor again?" she thought. Natalie, gritting her teeth, slid down from the rubble, feeling a burning sting in her thigh accompanied by the crack of fabric. Something snapped in her back as she straightened up, and the lighter fell to the ground with a soft clang. The grimace on her face froze.

- Fuck - she said.

Natalie's hands moved down, combing the floor like creatures living in the darkness near the seabed.

Her finger touched something cold. She tightened her hand on the rectangular object and picked it up. After a moment, the orange glow spread over her face and the nearby surroundings. Plop. Plop. Plop. Another sound interrupted the peaceful, repeated dripping. Natalie's attention snapped down the corridor, a monotonous hum seeping from somewhere inside. She released a quiet groan, tightening her hand on her thigh as she limped towards the door. A trace of blood decorated the floor beneath her.

The hum intensified, accompanied by metallic grating sounds. Natalie stood frozen, lighter held out in front. A loud bang reverberated through the corridor as the doorknob on her right shot out, and the door creaked open. Her heart raced, pounding harder and harder. The hum returned, and something small and metallic emerged behind the open door.

An attempt to step back turned into a stumble as her thigh refused to cooperate. Red afterimages flooded her vision with each blink. "What the fuck is this? A toy car?" Natalie thought, her gaze fixed on the metal creature within the pool of light emitted by the gasoline lighter. Her free hand, seeking support, reached toward the wall. As she touched the cold surface, memories of the horrors that had spread on the walls flooded back, and Natalie recoiled, rolling her arm back.

A beam of light flooded her from somewhere in the robot, which was moving towards Natalie. The metal tubes glittered with light reflections, making the robot shimmer with yellow, white, and orange.

The grating of a stone sometimes interrupted the monotonous hum of the caterpillar tracks when he passed over it.

- Robot? - Natalie said.

"This is something new. Why am I hallucinating about a robot?" she thought and backed away. She groaned, tightening her hand on her thigh, feeling the warm, sticky fluid under her fingers. She turned around, feeling an explosion of pain fill her leg. A scream escaped her lips, and she fell to the ground.

****

She opened her eyes and, leaning on her hands, noticed that the corridor was empty again. The last door on the left was now open, and a dim glow from within lit the nearby walls. Natalie stood up, stared at the light, and began to walk towards it. As she got closer, the warm golden glow caressed her skin. The scent in the air wrapped around her like a long-lost embrace, flooding her senses with the warmth and pleasure of past moments.

- Daniel! - she said.

With a few agile movements, she crossed the distance like a leopardess and stood in the doorway, bathed in a golden glow. Squinting her eyes, she entered the interior filled with golden light.

The clatter of the metal floor greeted her and continued, echoing with every step Natalie took. Dirty, moldy tiles were hanging off the walls. Those that were still on them, the rest were broken and scattered on the floor like bones in a devastated ossuary. She saw a copper bathtub with decorative metal lion paws at the end of the room.

The smell from the corridor here was even more robust. "Daniel's scent," she thought as she walked towards the bathtub. She passed two copper sinks covered in reddish-yellow sediment, filled with brown ooze that bubbled from time to time.

On the other side, she saw a toilet bowl from which water the color of mud and honey poured out in a thin stream, filling the bowl to the brim. A black leather wallet floated on the surface. Natalie's eyes fell on the leather object. "Good thing I don't have to get this out," she thought.

The closer she got, the more the weight in her chest pressed her to the floor. Standing beside the bathtub, she covered her mouth, suppressing a scream. Inside the bathtub, a stained bath curtain whose colors might have once been green and pink covered an uneven and sagging twisted form.

Natalie stopped the vomit rising in her throat and closed her eyes. Her chest was moving fast. A loud ringing and thumping spread in her head. Her trembling hand moved towards the curtain. The closer she got, the harder Natalie's heart beat.

She tore off the curtain.

- My God!

Shriveled head, clenched eyelids. Deformed holes in the place of the nose and blackened teeth protruding as if biting the lower lip that was no longer there. Stretched parchment-like skin, covered with a web of veins, highlighted every bone and rotten muscle—all the sharpness and curves of human physiognomy. Clothes hidden the rest.

And it was the sight of the clothes that was most shocking for Natalie. Dirty pants, stained in many places, and a wet, slimy shred that used to be a T-shirt. Despite the changes that had occurred, she recognized Daniel's clothes. She covered her mouth, trying to stop the scream and everything that would come after it.

The dried corpse's eyelids snapped open, white eyes boring into her.
- Give me a kiss, puffball - the corpse said.
Sharp as nails scraping on a chalkboard, laughter exploded in the room. Natalie jumped on her feet and ran out of the bathroom, chased by the creepy cackle.
Without slowing down, she hit the door of the opposite room, which creaked open. Natalie almost fell into a large hole that took up most of the place. She grabbed the doorknob and fell on the floor. The corpse's laughter was still echoing in her head, so she closed the door and leaned against it, her lungs burned.
Orange light emanated from the hole's depths as if a huge bonfire was burning underneath. A soft crunching sounded from inside the hole. After a while, Natalie saw an ant the size of a German shepherd crawling from inside. The chitinous exoskeleton gleamed with the warm color of the light flowing from below. The ant exited the hole and headed towards a rustic mahogany chair that wasn't there a moment ago. The ant sat on a chair with its abdomen tucked up, swayed its antennae, and tilted her head.

- Hello, Natalie - the ant said. - Daniel is waiting for you.
Go down the stairs on your left and then follow your heart.
Remember, never give up on your dreams, and let the power of
love guide you.
Natalie looked in the direction indicated. A faint glow illuminated
the stairs. Something she thought she would never see again.
The glow of sunlight.

She looked back at the ant who was now sitting on the lap of a
woman who looked like J. Whistler's mother from the painting
"Whistler's Mother." The woman looked at Natalie and put her
finger to her lips with her eyes pointing to the curled-up ant.
Even melodious snoring echoed throughout the room.

Natalie stood up, holding the door. She bowed to the woman
without knowing why and moved towards the stairs with her
back pressed against the wall. The hole was so close that the tops
of Natalie's feet stuck out just above it. She held her breath, afraid
the slightest twitch would throw her into the abyss.

She reached the steps, feeling the breeze on her face, and
descended towards the light.

Chapter Nine.

Natalie stood in the meadow. The wheat-colored grass touched her calves, and the wind brushed her cheeks, making her smile. The sky above her made Natalie want to lie down and stare at this work of nature. Glide with the clouds in the soft unconcern that seemed so tempting now. Human silhouettes loomed in the distance, twitching and dancing.

Her feet moved. The grass gave way in front of her as she ran toward the waving bunch of people that was beginning to take shape. A few meters in front of her, naked people were dancing, clasping their hands in a circle, moving in strange, jolted dance that looked like spasms. Daniel stood in the middle of the human circle, his skin glistening in the light. Natalie dashed. She stared at Daniel, feeling a pang in her chest and a heat in her stomach. She could now see his face, nose, mouth, and eyes. Eyes that were closed, unaware of her presence.

A pillar of light shot from the sky, blinding her and washing out the colors and shapes around her. The flash knocked her to the ground. A burning smudge of white spread under her clenched eyelids. When she opened her eyes again, quavering multi-colored circles of afterimages shot out everywhere she looked.

The blurry spot that was Daniel floated up in the center of the light that pierced the sky. Natalie uttered his name, her words coming out in a shaky breath. She rose from the ground and ran towards the light, eyes narrowed.

The circle broke up. The people jumped up and down, waving their arms. Bathed in terrifying brightness, they began to writhe, choke, and scream. They grabbed their heads and fell to their knees. Others trembled as if electrocuted.
The bodies became covered with scabs, blisters, and bulbous growths. Pulsating humps. No noses. Eyes that disappear under the skin. Hands that resemble the roots of dead trees. As if under an inaudible command, they turned their deformed bodies towards Natalie. She couldn't stop, running straight into the horrible crowd. Twisted arms with bony claws reached out toward her.

Natalie stopped feeling the ground under her boots. She felt the breeze replace the warmth of the soil as it flowed over her. The deformed revelers shrank in her eyes, losing their shapes.
The rush of air whipped her body and crashed into her face, and the pillar of light grew until it filled her entire field of vision. Inside, the dark spot began to retake shape, and Natalie stretched her arms out to it. She broke through the curtain of brightness, and her fingers felt the skin and bone of Daniel's ankle.
Sudden pull. Pressure on the calf. Then, the same on the other leg. Daniel blurred again, disappearing into the luminous prison.

Natalie turned her head. Something flesh-like, covered with rust-colored mucus, spots, and veins, wrapped around her legs.

Wrinkled, slimy, baggy ropes dragged her down. Two revelers were lying on the ground, and ropes of intestines were coming out from their torn stomachs, dragging her down.
The ground rumbled. Natalie lay curled up, her quivering body filled with internal heat. She was surrounded on all sides by the twisted, bulbous persons who were getting closer with every second. A tug at her hair sprang Natalie up to her knees, pain lancing through her head. Natalie saw the swollen like in someone who drowned, the scarred face of Ethan's wife.
- Hello, Natalie - Not-Mary said.
The exhale from her gaping, twisted mouth was like the deepest depths of sewage. Natalie's stomach churned, a slow, nauseating build-up before she vomited. She teetered on the edge of consciousness, but the world spun into darkness.

A sharp sting radiated across her cheek. Not-Mary's hand then hit Natalie's other cheek. She opened her watery eyes wide, staring at the disgusting caricature of Mary.
- Don't sleep, bitch! You don't want to miss the grand finale - Not-Mary said.
"Aunt! Aunt!" came a squeaky unison from under Not-Mara's head. Natalie looked at the swollen body, covered in scabs and peeling skin. Two heads emerged in place of the breasts, barely visible behind the bloated veins. Gray, round faces with pig eyes snapped their toothy jaws, and thick saliva gushed from them.
- Oh, someone wants to say hello to you - Not-Mary said, pushing Natalie's head down.

She felt the pressure bringing her closer to the wriggling heads, hearing the jaws clicking faster and faster. Natalie freed herself from the grab with a hit of her hand and jumped away.

Her trembling body was lit by a red flame that spread throughout her body, leaving only her face visible. Natalie watched as the burning flames danced across her. The fire crackled as it spread across her back, chest, and limbs. The eyes of the revelers who had them reflected the bloody glow of the blast. A wave of fire erupted from Natalie's body, burning everything in its path, and the screams of those gathered rose towards the sky along with the smoke. Tongues of fire lashed out like whips, catching fleeing people. Living torches spread across the meadow and soon drop convulsed.

Wrapped in flames, Not-Mary leapt towards Natalie. The crackling of the flames was accompanied by the hiss of melting fat from the fingers wrapped around her neck. A black, writhing body pressed its fingers against Natalie's throat. A few sharper pops sounded as the fingers fell like broken matches.

A blast of fire blew Not-Mary away. She crawled on the remains of her knees towards the pillar of light. The outstretched arm fell off, followed by fragments of the back and face. The black remains of Not-Mary now lay motionless, covered in a shroud of flames.

The meadow turned into a lake of fire filled with burning, blackened corpses twisted by the temperature. Blackness obscured the view as the rising smoke shrouded Natalie and carried her away. Smoke and fire remained in the background for the pillar of light that spread across her face. Natalie's eyes squeezed shut without her help as a brightness washed over her, obscuring everything else. A piercing voice like thunder echoed in her head.

  - DANIEL IS READY. YOU CAN TAKE HIM BACK NOW - light said.

Chapter Ten.

Amid the surrounding darkness, a soft, rhythmic sound made its way into Natalie's consciousness. Plop. Plop. Plop.

Her eyes widened. Spasms of pain spread across her thigh almost as fast as her heartbeat. Shallow, uncontrollable breaths squeezed her chest like hot hoops. She gritted her teeth and dug her fingers into the floor, trying to get up.

Any movement brought on nausea, and her thigh protested every attempt at movement by sending shocking stabs to the brain. A few muffled screams scattered through the walls as Natalie finally rose to her feet. A shaky wrist movement and a metallic click made an orange light flash from the lighter.

The wavering flame cast her shadow against the wall, reminding Natalie of the bio-horrors on the walls. With her other hand, she squeezed her thigh and moved towards the door behind which she had met an ant in her dream.

Each step felt like a hammer blow, the heat in her thigh burning hotter and hotter, flooding her mind. Her uneven breathing echoed through the walls as she continued her slow walk in the chosen direction. Balancing her body, she put her weight on her good leg. The illuminated door revealed peeling paint curling in places where it hadn't fallen off yet.

She kept replaying the words from her dream, "DANIEL IS READY. YOU CAN TAKE HIM BACK NOW."
 She pushed the door, feeling the cold wood bit into her hand. "Please, no holes. Please. Please, no holes," she thought as she entered the room. Natalie illuminated the interior.

She saw the rough concrete floor, a small rectangular hole at the bottom of the wall, and, to her left, stairs leading down.
She headed to the steps. She stood in front of the stairs leading down and turned around, seeing the outline of an empty mahogany chair at the back of the room.
She climbed the first step and stepped back when she saw the walls in the warm light of the lighter. There wasn't the slightest inch of free space on them. Everything was covered with growths from which thousands of thin white branches sprouted.
They even spread along some of the steps, looking like white earthworms crawling out of the darkness. Flashes of childhood memories filled her head.
She was again a twelve-year-old sent by her mother to get something from the basement. It didn't matter that the basement was well-lit, with white walls covered with posters from movies that no one remembers anymore. The moment when she had to descend into this abyss containing everything that her young mind could create now came back to her. The parent's words, "The basement is the same place as any other place in the house," did not alleviate the paralysis that held back Natelie's feet. "There's not an ordinary basement waiting for me there, but maybe Daniel is," she thought.

She tightened her fingers on her burning thigh and began her slow descent into the depths of the mansion. A sour odor mixed with something sweet filled her nostrils. In the wavering light, the growths seemed to undulate like a vast network whose complex patterns stretched on over and over.

Some reminded Natalie of feathers, delicate and thin. In contrast, with bulbous tips sticking out like hands reaching for her. Their colors ranged from pale white to deeper shades of yellow and brown, opalescent in the light she carried like Prometheus.

Threadlike growths cracked under her boots, others just bent, soft and resilient. Natalie felt like she was walking on the back of some enormous creature that either did not want to or could not wake up. Descended staggered, stopping every few steps. The pulsing in her ears grew stronger. On her fingertips clenched on her thigh, she felt a warm stickiness. The blood on her hand glistened in the light with zigzagging reflections. The lower she went, the more growths surrounded her, rustling and creaking under the pressure of her thick, hard soles. A strange odor seemed to permeate her with each breath she took.

The stairs ended, leaving her on the threshold of a vast chamber that more resembled a bizarre garden than something built by human hands. As far as she could see in the dim light, growths in thick layers enveloped the floor and walls. Uneven, bulbous, twisted, and intricate shapes formed a biological mosaic that consumed every bit of space.

Stumbling over coiled and sprawling irregularities, she moved forward amidst endless rustles and cracks under her feet. Natalie reached the center of the chamber and fell to her knees with a scream frozen on her parted lips. The earth beneath had risen, cracking and tearing the once sturdy floor.

From these fissures grew two massive pillar-like plant formations that dominated everything else with their presence. Emerging from the torn floor and reaching up to the ceiling, which Natalie could barely discern. Their smooth surfaces dazzled with whiteness, shifting to a flesh-like orange at the biological crown covered with tentacle-like protrusions.

The colossal pillars seemed to be the epicenter of the monstrous growths that had become the mansion's new owners. As much as Natalie could make out, countless tentacle-like vines of the growths extended from them outward. Like parents and protectors, the monstrous, swollen pillars looked down upon their endless offspring. She knelt still, absorbing the enormity of the transformation the room must have undergone, allowing at the same time the weird charm and peace of the place she found herself in to seep into her mind. She felt as if she had entered the lair of a creature never discovered by science or stumbled upon an ancient sanctuary forever changed by the relentless passage of time and the unyielding grip of these mysterious growths.

Then, her gaze rested on something that did not fit in with everything else. In front of the biological pillars, on a tangle of bulbs, outgrowths, and long tentacle-like vines, Natalie spotted the outline of a human back.

Choking and coughing, she moved forward, supporting her aching leg. Her body gave in, collapsing next to the curled-up, unconscious Daniel. Exhausted like never before. Overwhelmed by a weight that filled her, she lay next to him, illuminating the motionless Daniel.

She wanted to say, "I found you," but instead, a tearing pain induced a cough from deep within her. Her lungs, throat, and nostrils felt like scorching ash. Trembling from the relentless cough, she moved closer to him with the last of her strength. Darkness embraced them. "We are together again," she thought, and everything blurred into wonderful oblivion.

***

- Natalie - Daniel whispered.
Natalie opened her eyes. She didn't know how much time had passed. It seemed as if she had been lying there for ages.
Daniel was still unconscious.
"We won't get out of here," she thought.
- But this damn thing will die here, too - Natalie said.
She got to her knees. Natalie slid off her backpack and probed out a bottle. She drank. The inner fire dimmed. Natalie stood up. She threw the bottle, which shattered with a clink somewhere at the base of the pillars, scattering its contents. The sharp smell of alcohol mixed with the peculiar odor of the place.
She looks in the dark for a metal object on one of the outgrowths. A circle of light surrounded them, and Natalie looked at Daniel.

Everything stood still for a fraction of a second, and the chamber seemed to hold its breath. The lighter followed the path of the bottle. A crackling sound filled the room as the growths caught fire, causing the flames to dance and swirl.

The blue flame that began to consume the pillars was replaced by a deep, juicy red. Stale air, filled with gases accumulated over the years, and spores filled the chamber, intensifying the effect. The fire burst out of the pillars like a violent flood. The labyrinth of tendrils and nematodeslike fingers emanating from them distributed the flames along a series of connections. Hungry and relentless, tongues of fire raced along them. Glowing in incredible shades of green and blue, different parts of the growths began to burn. Just moments ago, this place was a kingdom of silence and shadow.

Now torn apart by infernal sounds. Screeches, crackles, and hisses filled the chamber, as did the multicolored waves of fire. The walls seemed alive, vibrating from the heat and light. The central pillars looked like torches, directing the wrath of fire into every corner. Natalie stepped back, watching the captivating dance of destruction, the flames licking and writhing in their wild hunger. The energy of the fire destroyed the oppressive atmosphere, its heat replaced the cold and damp embrace of the underground chamber.

Natalie landed on the burning floor as a sudden blast swept over her. The roar filled her head, and smoke filled her lungs.

Her mind urged her to flee, but Natalie only wanted to be with
Daniel. She turned around. She pushed herself up on her arms.
She couldn't see him.

- Daniel! - Heat filled her lungs.
The flames had already covered everything within sight.
She looked towards the stairs.

She couldn't see him there either, but the path to them wasn't
cut off yet. Her arms gave way beneath her. Her body seemed to
merge with the surroundings. The touch of heat tore her skin
like hooks, pulling in all directions. The sounds of the burning
growths resonated like the screams of ancient creatures.
The blazing pillars shot jets of fire. An outcry filled the chamber.
The cascades of flames and shapes forming on them resembled a
leviathan emerging from the sun's core only to perish in an
all-ending explosion.

Chapter Eleven.

Consciousness came in waves, pulling her from the depths of
darkness. A rhythmic beeping greeted her ears before she opened
her eyes. When she did, the bright fluorescent light streaming
from the ceiling made her squint, twisting her mouth.
Gone was the underground chamber's atmosphere, replaced by
the sterile scent of antiseptic agents. She felt a soft mattress
beneath her and a snow-white duvet wrapped around her, which
lay a fluffy blanket. The window to her left showed a small
fragment of the outside world.

The warming sun, clouds moving, tall buildings, and the fading
sounds of passing cars. A small plastic package lay on one of the
chairs in the back of the room. The walls were adorned with
cheap, generic prints in plastic frames suitable for any interior: a
landscape depicting an empty beach, a close-up of a rose touched
by dew.

Natalie was connected by tubes to the buzzing equipment beside
her bed. Her last memory was of all-consuming flames and
piercing heat. She wanted to jump out of the comfortable bed, but
a few deep breaths calmed her mind. Her throat, chest, and the
rest of her body throbbed with pain, but not as big as before.

Dryness in her throat. Saliva didn't pass through her throat as it should, causing Natalie to exert the muscles responsible for this process. "Stylopharyngeal muscles? Was that what it was called?" she thought, surprised by the clarity and ease with which this came to her. "Or perhaps pharyngeal?" The bedsheet rustled under her as she tried to sit up, but an overwhelming heaviness pinned her back to the bed. "Well, look at that, they're getting cleverer," she thought. She turned her head towards the window.

- You're not frightening me with fucked up visions but with the prospect that I can get well again! - Natalie said.
One of the machines beeped faster. Staring out the window, she recalled the events preceding her awakening, which now seemed like a distant dream. In the room, there was only the quiet beeping and the rustle of her restless movements in the bed.
"What if this isn't another nightmare? What if I really am in a hospital?" she wondered, staring out the window.

Natalie heard a soft creak of the door. A figure stood in the entrance, its silhouette surrounded by the bright light of the corridor. A petite woman with gray hair entered the room.
Still foggy and restless, Natalie's mind struggled with chaotic memories, trying to piece them together. The woman approached, worry lines forming on her face and moist, hazel eyes looking at the lying Natalie. Those eyes sparked a flood of memories. Laughter from childhood, tender hugs, and bedtime story reading. Love and care were reflected in that face, now approaching Natalie.

- Mom? - she whispered.

Her mother's eyes, clouded with worry and sadness, were now filled with tears. They shone, expressing a mix of relief and concern.

- Natalie - she said with a trembling voice.

At that moment, the weight in Natalie's head, a constant tangle of turmoil and anxiety, lessened. The woman stroked her daughter's face with a calm and comforting touch. Mixed tears of joy and relief streamed down the cheeks of both mother and daughter.

- What happened? - Natalie said.

- A fire. There was a fire. - the woman swallowed her tears.

- They found you in some old house.

As she tried to rise, the veins in Natalie's arms swelled. She felt overwhelming weakness and fell back onto the bed.

- No. Don't get up - the woman said, leaning over her daughter and touching her wet forehead. - You need to lie down. I'll go get a doctor - she said.

Her mother stood up, heading for the door. Natalie stirred in the bed.

- Mom. Who was with me?

The woman turned back to her with reddened eyes.

- Some couple called the fire department and ambulance. And Ethan said he helped you and Daniel get out of...

- Daniel! Ethan! What about them? Where are they? - Natalie said.

A burst of coughing filled the room. Natalie's mother handed her a cup of water.

- Slowly, darling - she said, helping her sit up enough to reach the styrofoam cup. - You'll find out everything, but a doctor must first see you. Please, try to calm down. I'll be right back.

With tears welling up, Natalie looked at her.
- Tell me, please. I need to know.
The woman, looking at her daughter's face, injured and irritated by the heat, spoke with a soft voice.
- Ethan is fine. He was examined and has gone home. Daniel. It's worse with Daniel, but the doctor said he'll make it through.
- Thank you - Natalie said.
- Rest. I'll be right back.
Natalie tried to rise again, twisting her mouth in pain and falling back onto the bed. The woman rushed to her.
- Lie down. Lie down, darling.
Natalie reached out her arms.
- Please hold me, Mom.
Natalie felt the warmth of her hug, accompanied by a comfort she thought she would never feel again.
- I'm sorry - Natalie said with a breaking voice.
- For what, darling?
Natalie looked into her eyes.
- I'm sorry for being a bad daughter.

Epilogue.

Shadows moved across the ceiling in the dim light of dawn, and the noise of the city starting a new day came in from outside the window. Natalie arched in a stretch, the indentations in the mattress caressing her, encouraging further rest. She yawned, nestled in the bed that was her cocoon of softness and warmth. It cradled her in its delicate embrace, almost as if it wanted to comfort her. She turned over, the rumpled bedding marking Daniel's sleeping spot. "He's already up," she thought, but she didn't feel like getting up herself.

Physically, she felt much better. But the emotional scars ran deeper and, despite the passage of time, still lurked on the edges of her consciousness like a phantom weed entrenched in her brain, refusing to be uprooted.

A smile appeared on her lips when she thought of Daniel. His unwavering support had been her rock. How he held her every time she woke up screaming in the night. The certainty in his voice. The warmth of his touch. All of this had played a significant role in her healing. She got up, threw on his pale yellow stretched sweater, and walked to the living room. A small room brightened by white walls and large windows framing the balcony doors.

The distant hum of everyday life spread inside.
A beechwood bookshelf filled with books against one wall and a black sofa opposite. On it was the book Daniel started reading two weeks ago, "The End of Nossrefey" by Woodrow Camoran. Natalie glanced at the closed door of the darkroom before turning her gaze back to the balcony. Through the blinds, the outline of a figure was visible. The open balcony door beckoned to the other side. 'He'll catch a cold,' she thought, opening the door wider.

Daniel stood with his back to her. She drew her eyes to his bent arms resting on the railing. The whiteness of his clenched fingers contrasted with the red seeping out from under his nails.
She looked at his head. Something protruded from his open mouth. Natalie closed her eyes, the biological nightmare from the underground chamber flooding her thoughts. She smiled.
Her lifted eyelids revealed the empty gaze of white eyes.
- At last, we live again - she said.

THE END.

NIGHTMARES UNDER THE MANSION

H. P. Perlowski

26.11.2023

Thank you for reading this book.

For more information about new books,
comics, and other creations please visit the website:

https://hpperlowski.com/

Contact:

paul@hpperlowski.com

https://hpperlowski.com/?page_id=58

www.ingramcontent.com/pod-product-compliance
Lightning Source LLC
LaVergne TN
LVHW051053180726
843512LV00019B/1462